The Deception

ARIES

fore the last

I scrambled forward, jumped to my feet.

And turned to find Chapman pointing the gun at me. With him, a Hork-Bajir bodyguard. The Hork-Bajir stepped forward.

"Wait!" Chapman grinned. "I think I will take you prisoner instead. My own personal prisoner of war. But just to make sure you don't try to break out. . ."

Bam!

I fell to the floor.

Chapman locked the door behind him.

> **Even the book morphs!**
> **Flip the pages**
> **and check it out!**

Look for other ANIMORPHS titles
by K.A. Applegate:

ANIMORPHS

The Deception

K.A. Applegate

SCHOLASTIC

Scholastic Children's Books,
Commonwealth House, 1–19 New Oxford Street,
London WC1A 1NU, UK
a division of Scholastic Ltd
London ~ New York ~ Toronto ~ Sydney ~ Auckland
Mexico City ~ New Delhi ~ Hong Kong

First published in the USA by Scholastic Inc., 2000
First published in the UK by Scholastic Ltd, 2001

ISBN 0 439 99364 4

Printed and bound in Great Britain by Cox & Wyman Ltd, Reading, Berks.

10 9 8 7 6 5 4 3 2 1

The author wishes to thank Elise Donner for her assistance in preparing this manuscript.

For Dad

For Michael and Jake

Chapter 1

"This is the resistance."

I had never heard more pride in Prince Jake's voice. I know I had never been more proud of him.

<Yes, and what is it you want? How is it you are communicating with us?>

Clearly, the Andalite officer on the other end of our interplanetary connection was not similarly impressed.

Rachel snorted. Jake shot a look at her before speaking. "Look," he said, "we don't have much time here. This transmission could be tracked. And we have a lot to talk about. First, the Anatiworld situation, it's a trap. The Yeerks have constructed huge Dracon cannon sites on all the moons. Your fleet goes there, it's obliterated."

There was a moment of silence. An understandable delay, given the enormous distance over which we were transmitting and the primitiveness of our transmitting device.

But I suspected the silence meant something else.

<We know of your situation on Earth, human.> The voice belonged to another Andalite. Its tone suggested an officer superior to the one with whom Jake had just spoken.

"Yes," Jake began, "but things have changed. We—"

<We know that you are in need of our assistance.>

"Rude," Marco mumbled. "Let a guy finish his sentence."

The voice went on, cold and imperious. An Andalite's voice. <And we must consider the possibility that you would lie to us in an effort to become our top priority.>

"What the. . .?"

Cassie grabbed Rachel's arm, motioned for her to be silent.

"Look," Jake said, controlled anger making his voice tense. "We've got the information on good authority. And you have no reason to suspect us of double-dealing."

"Yes he does." Marco again. "We're puny, backward humans. Not great, honourable Andalites."

<Prince Jake, if I may?>

Jake nodded and I stepped forward, closer to the still unperfected device.

Since coming to this faraway planet, I have spoken to my people on several occasions.

Once, via adjustments I made to a primitive human radio telescope. Adjustments that allowed me to break into Zero-space.

Once, on an Andalite ship commanded by the traitor Samilin-Corrath-Gahar.

On two other occasions, I have conversed with Andalites who had also come to Earth.

But this — this was different. Everything was different. The war was escalating. The Andalites, my people, had to listen to us. They had to be *made* to listen.

<This is Aximili-Esgarrouth-Isthill,> I said. <What my prince says is correct. Our source for the information regarding the Anati planet comes from none other than Visser One, originator of the Yeerk invasion on this planet. Visser One was sent to build the Anati defences and to draw the Andalite fleet. Recently the visser returned to Earth. We eliminated the Yeerk and liberated the host. This is the truth.>

<That'll show them,> Tobias said. Tobias — my *shorm*, a *nothlit*. Our lookout.

What came next I had not expected. Later, I wondered why, with my varied experience of Andalite character, I had not entertained the

3

possibility of my own people's suspicion and neglect.

<The high command will consider your words,> the officer replied. <The brother of War Prince Elfangor always deserves to be heard. However . . . in our opinion, and given his record to date, it is also possible that Aximili-Esgarrouth-Isthill has confused his loyalties.>

<I. . .>

But it was too late to protest.

<Bug fighters!> Tobias. <Get out of there, now!>

"Everybody, morph! Go, go go!"

Our transmission had gone on too long. The Yeerks were now coming in for the capture. Or the kill.

I should have paid more attention to the time.

TSSEEEWWW!

"Ax!" Jake shouted. "I said, run! Grab the transponder and haul butt!"

<Cop cars coming, guys! We've got human-Controllers with gun permits on the way!> Tobias shouted. <Hurry!>

TSSEEEWWW! TSSEEEWWW!

The sand around us turned to glass under the awful heat and pressure of Dracon fire. The midnight surf boiled and coughed up dead sea life.

And in the long, coarse beach grass, under

cover of the dim crescent moon, Rachel, Cassie, Marco and Jake rapidly morphed to their standard bird-of-prey morphs.

For the usual security reasons they could not be identified by the Yeerks as human. In Marco's case, he could not be identified by the Yeerks as alive.

<Out of here.> Rachel flapped massive bald-eagle wings in the cool night air and struggled off the ground.

Cassie and Marco, each gone osprey, followed.

<Ax? Tobias?> Jake yelled. <Don't let them get the transponder!>

A peregrine falcon rose into the night.

TSSEEEWWW! TSSEEEWWW!

I tucked the transponder to my chest, bent as low as I could and still be stable, and ran. In the direction of the dunes, not the car park. . .

<Whoa! Ax-man, look out!>

Over the damp sand two policemen came slipping and sliding, handheld Dracon beams aimed — at me.

"Andalite scum! Halt!"

"Tsseeer!"

"Aaargh!"

One human-Controller down, raked across the eyes by a red-tailed hawk.

And before the other could blink. . .

Fwap!

5

I lifted my tail over my shoulder and hit him with the flat of the blade. He was definitely down. And out.

Chapter 2

My name is Aximili-Esgarrouth-Isthill. I am an Andalite. Son of Noorlin-Sirinial-Coorat and Forlay-Esgarrouth-Maheen. Younger brother of celebrated War Prince Elfangor-Sirinial-Shamtul. An *aristh*, a cadet, a warrior in training.

But my existence in the group of humans that calls itself the Animorphs has, I believe, qualified me as a full warrior. An experienced fighter.

Why do I fight for and with a people not my own? Because, in many ways, these humans *have* become my own.

And the central, most important reason is that the humans are fighting off an invasion of an evil, parasitic alien species known as the Yeerks. The Yeerks must be stopped.

7

It doesn't matter who stops them, or why. Maybe, just maybe, it doesn't even matter how.

But that is a dangerous question to ponder.

Better to concentrate on the present. And the most important thing we needed to do was to stop Visser Three from being promoted to the powerful position of Visser One.

Because as Visser One, nothing would stop him from an all-out invasion of planet Earth.

And now, after the frustrating communication with the Andalite officer, it looked as if our task would be a much more difficult one than we'd already anticipated.

This fact, along with the fact that in the eyes of the human world he was dead, made Marco somewhat — cranky.

He, Tobias and I were relaxing in my scoop the morning following the disaster at the beach. My advanced technical ability had provided me with a full variety of cable packages, free of charge. Marco was in possession of the wonderful invention Tobias had found for me — a remote.

"Freakin' nothing on! Hundreds of stations and nothing — *nothing!* — worth watching."

<Marco?> Tobias sat perched on the arm of a chair Marco had dragged to the scoop from what he described as "some dump".

"What?"

<Give me the remote.>

8

Marco stood and tossed the device on to the seat of the chair.

"You know what really gets me?" he said.

I did not reply. I have long ago learned that humans often ask what are known as "rhetorical questions". When they ask such questions, they do not really want or need you to answer. They are prepared to answer for you.

"I'll tell you what really gets me," Marco said, pacing. "Here we are, six semi-freaks busting our butts trying to prevent a full-scale alien invasion of Earth and I bet you dollars to doughnuts. . ."

Tobias cocked his head. <Something your grandmother used to say?>

Marco glared. "I'd bet a million bucks if I had it that if the average guy on the street was told he'd better get ready, there was going to be a major war, he'd just laugh. He wouldn't even believe a full-scale war was possible any more! The average person is too content."

<Would you prefer a general state of panic?> I said. It was a rhetorical question.

"My point is just that people are complacent. All-out, global warfare is a thing of the past. That's what people think, anyway. No one wants it, no one's ready for it. And who's going to believe Earth is about to be attacked by aliens from outer space? They'd think a call to arms was just a publicity stunt for the *X Files* or something."

<Marco has a point,> Tobias said. <Particularly Americans. I mean, we've got no enemies at sea, not many on land, and those aren't exactly real scary. The country's just not ready for war. Maybe it's arrogance, maybe a combination of things, but the average person on the street just doesn't think another world war is possible.>

<So if we were to go public with our information or alert certain authorities. . .>

Marco snorted and flopped into his chair. "We'd be seriously deep in it."

". . .*the Council suggests . . . bzzsmmm. . .*"

I swung my stalk eyes towards the small laptop in one corner of my scoop. A new model Apple computer I had acquired at *PC World*. With the help of several months of Rachel's credit-card allowance.

She informed me that I owed her "big time" for her assistance.

"What the heck was that?"

I raised a hand to silence Marco. Nothing further came from the computer.

<I believe that was a snippet of a Yeerk dialogue,> I explained finally. <I have applied a computer program of my own making to the Zero-space transponder I created — with help from your father, Marco.>

I have always believed in giving credit where credit is due. Even if it was to a human.

<And?> Tobias stared at me with his intense hawk gaze.

<And,> I continued, <this program attempts to decode locally originated Z-space transmissions. Unfortunately, and through no possible fault of my own,> I admitted, <the success rate of the program is less than thirty per cent. Human computer technology is simply too slow to overcome advanced Yeerk encoding in a reliable and consistent way.>

"But the success part, Ax," Marco pressed. "The fifteen or twenty per cent of the time something does get through, that's something. Or could be."

I nodded. Another human gesture I have acquired.

<Yes.>

". . .again the Council of Thirteen commends Visser Two on his proposed plan, which we have designated Operation 9466: Phase One. Pending final approval from Visser One, the Council orders Visser Two to proceed as . . . bzzmss . . . gerubzz. . ."

There was silence. Andalite, human and *nothlit* — each of us was, I believe it is fair to say, stunned.

Chapter 3

<**O**K, I'm not the only one who heard that, am I?>

Tobias continued to stare at the now silent computer.

Marco sank back into his chair.

"You know what I love about this life? There's never a dull moment. Freakin' never."

<I believe the most important question now is: who has become Visser One? We are responsible for the death of the Yeerk that was in that position. Not Visser Three. He can't have been promoted after botching a Council-ordered execution!>

<Not even to the rank of Visser Two?> Tobias said. <Why not? I don't understand Yeerk politics. Do you?>

Marco stood up again. "Look, let's assume our old buddy is now either Visser One or Two. Who's left? And what's Operation 9466?"

Suddenly, I felt angry and frustrated.

<If only I had access to a more advanced technology! Then I would be able to intercept the entire Yeerk communication. I would. . .>

Marco laughed. It sounded somewhat like a dog's bark.

"Hey, Ax-man, ease up on us dopey humans, OK? Besides, that machine you've got there is, like, a toy. For the lay person. What an intellectual Andalite giant like you wants is to hack into some major government computer system."

<Even though it's illegal,> Tobias added. <Not sure I'd advise it.>

It was a very good idea. Illegal. But we were at war. We didn't have a choice.

<Yes, excellent,> I said. <We need information. We must do whatever we can to get it.>

"Whoa. Just, whoa." Marco. "I wasn't actually suggesting we break into the US government's personal stash. That's the kind of invasion of privacy that gets you life. In jail."

<What are you saying?>

Marco rolled his eyes. An unfortunate and unattractive expression.

"I'm saying it's illegal. Dangerous. I'm saying it's wrong. Not right."

13

Humans are an odd species. They will proclaim a particular ethical and moral stance one day. And the next, they will proclaim an opposite stance with equal passion.

When pressed, they explain such behaviour as caused by "different circumstances". Also, depending on "the situation".

<Marco,> I said, <I seem to recall you telling your father recently that nothing is "right" any more. That stealing in the name of the cause is one of your specialities. That when the war is over and there is a "right" again, you will make amends.>

"Do you know how seriously annoying it is to quote someone's words back at them?" he shouted. "Do you?"

<Does that mean you agree with my plan?>

"It means I'll go along with it. Maybe we can figure out a deal, give the government boys something in return for what we're taking. Hey, Bird-boy? Are you with us?"

<If I said no, would it really make a difference? Would it stop you, Ax?>

Not a rhetorical question. <No,> I said, <it would not.>

In spite of Marco's earlier protests, he was the one who suggested we attempt to infiltrate the National Security Agency's code-breaking computer system.

And it was Marco who suggested that we

should also install a program able to crack any possible security code conceived by humans.

Needless to say, I would be the one to devise such a program. Which, in the next few moments, I did.

Now we were ready.

Tobias kept careful watch from above. Marco hung over my shoulder.

And with the aid of Cassie's mobile phone and my new lime-green iMac, I proceeded to reroute the Yeerk Z-space transmissions through the NSA's central computer.

"Federal prison," Marco said, "here we come."

<What's happening, Ax?>

<The NSA is trying to block my transmission. Now they are receiving my decoding program.>

A few keystrokes. A moment of tension. More waiting.

"Ax, what's going on!"

<The NSA has stopped blocking me. Now, let's see what we have here.>

<One thing, Ax-man,> Tobias called. <Uh, are you sure the program you sent these guys can't be used to decipher your own stuff? Or the Yeerks'?>

Slowly, I swung one eye stalk around and up to look at Tobias, perched on the branch of a tree.

<OK, OK, sorry I asked.>

15

And then, suddenly, it happened.

This bigger, faster, more powerful machine, combined with my superior Andalite technical knowledge and skills. . .

". . .*The newly appointed Visser One, recently Visser Three, current leader of the Yeerk mission on planet Earth . . . has approved Operation 9466. Visser Two has undertaken a journey to Earth to assist in the execution of this long-anticipated military action. . .*"

"Bingo," Marco whispered.

Chapter 4

<Visser One. Formerly Visser Three. Esplin 9466.>

It had come to me in a flash on our rapid trip to Cassie's barn. The Animorphs' traditional meeting place.

"Of course." Jake. "So, this mission is major. If it's being named after the reigning visser."

"And if the second in command, whoever he or she is, will be coming along for the ride," Rachel added.

"But what's the point?" Cassie asked.

"I'll give you one guess. Yes, that's right, boys and girls." Marco paced. "We know from my mother that our old nemesis has been pushing for all-out assault on Earth. No more sneaky,

17

middle-of-the-night stuff. Now we're gonna see major population 'cleansing'. You want to be one of us, a Yeerk? Fine. You don't? You're dead. The Yeerks don't need everyone. One billion people? More than enough."

<What are the Yeerks afraid of?> I asked.

Marco looked at me. "Two things. The Andalite fleet. And humanity's own resources. I'm talking weapons, but also ingenuity. Flexibility. Hope. All those traits the former Visser One acknowledged and respected and feared about us human beings. The traits the former Visser Three has always ignored."

"No way hope is going to conquer a huge alien force," Rachel said grimly. "At least not before being massacred."

Marco sighed. "I know."

"But the Yeerks don't," Jake added. "They also don't know for sure we aren't equipped weapon-wise to annihilate them if they attack. And they don't know for sure the chances of the Andalite fleet coming to Earth's rescue are less than good."

"I keep remembering those Yeerk forces we saw in for repair," Cassie said. "When we rescued Marco's mum. It's . . . it's beginning to feel overwhelming."

<Look. Whether or not the Yeerks know it, the truth is we have no space-based weapons.> Tobias, his voice flat. <We'll be slaughtered.

Remember what we saw of open warfare? Henry Five and the French. Washington on the Delaware. Normandy Beach. OK, those events were slightly distorted, but the blood was the same as when they really happened. The death was the same.>

"Both world wars and the plague all rolled into one. That's what we're facing." Marco's eyes were dark. "That kind of massive destruction."

Silence. The situation was not good.

Jake looked at me. "Ax. I want your honest opinion. Since that one transmission on the beach, we've heard nothing from the Andalites. Should we assume the fleet isn't coming? Should we go ahead on our own?"

What could I say? To answer such a question — with a "yes" or a "no" — would cast suspicion on my loyalty to my people.

The Andalites. And the humans.

If the Andalite fleet had chosen to ignore our warning and had moved to the Anati system, one of the new Visser One's conditions for all-out war had been met. We were in a situation of maximum danger.

One of my peoples had betrayed the other.

In spite of my admiration — and, yes, affection — for humans, I have always hoped my future would be on the home planet. With my parents. Perhaps even with Estrid-Corill-Darrath and a family of my own.

And yet — my experience with my birth

19

people since being stranded on planet Earth has been . . . complex. Less than one hundred per cent satisfactory.

Now — the chance of my ever returning and being welcomed with open arms seemed even smaller.

Particularly after the stinging words of doubt spoken by the anonymous Andalite officer.

"Ax?"

But it was not as if my experience with humans and their culture had been without disappointment. I had been saddened by human behaviour, disgusted even. By their incomprehensible violence towards one another.

Once we had been forced to chase Visser Four through history in order to retrieve the Time Matrix. To prevent the dawning of a world even more frightening than any horrible time that had come before.

Before that strange journey through centuries past, I thought I had come to understand humans. But as horrible scenes of carnage and terror unfolded before my eyes, I realized that I knew very little about human beings.

They could be insane, hate-filled creatures. I could make no sense of the outrageous violence, of the mindless killing.

And it frightened me.

But I had made friends. We were our own family. And this was still our fight.

I was Andalite. And, in a way, I was human.

"Ax. Do you think the Andalites are coming?"

<I do not know, Prince Jake,> I said, my eyes solemn. <I honestly do not know.>

Chapter 5

"OK. The Yeerks want Earth." Jake looked at each of us in turn. "Well, they can't have it."

"Look." Marco, musing. "Maybe the situation isn't as desperate as we think. Yet. Maybe the Yeerks are just seeing what they can get away with. They push, we push back. They don't try that particular move again. They shove, we don't shove back, they shove again, but this time, harder. And eventually, we fall on our butts."

Rachel nodded. "Right. We don't wait around for the cavalry. We fight with everything we've got, with or without the Andalites. Self-defence is always justified. We've known that from the beginning. End of story."

"Even when the odds are abysmal?" Cassie said, half to herself. "Maybe especially then."

<War is irrational,> I murmured, weary from

so much talk. From the thought of what lay ahead. <Though it is sometimes necessary.>

<Ax,> Tobias said, <show Jake those two sets of numbers we got from the transmission just before we left the scoop.>

<Of course.> I handed Jake the piece of paper on which Marco had written several bits of information.

Jake shook his head. "Longitude? Latitude? That's my guess."

"Mine, too." Marco retrieved an atlas he'd stashed in the hayloft. "And . . . let's see . . . this is strange. We're talking both sites over a thousand kilometres out to sea . . . but each site only thirty kilometres apart."

Rachel peered over Jake's shoulder. "Dates and times. Today." She checked her watch. "It's nine A.M. OK, these times are . . . seven, then nine hours from now. Four o'clock this afternoon, then six this evening."

Rachel stared in disbelief at me, Tobias and Marco. "Could you have shown us this any later?! Let's go!"

"Calm down," Jake said. "We can't do anything until we have some idea of what this information means. The middle of the ocean. Why? And what's going to happen? No clue."

"Except that it's got to be huge." Marco sighed dramatically. "And we've got to be there. The fate of the world and all."

"How do we get that far out to sea in less than seven hours?" Cassie said. "No morph is going to make it."

There was another heavy silence. I turned my main eyes towards Jake.

It is a huge responsibility for a young person, human or Andalite, to be a leader.

Finally, Jake spoke. His eyes were dull but his voice was firm.

"Things are different," he said. "From now on, we take what we need. We do what we have to do. No matter what the consequences."

"Jake. . ." Cassie began.

"There's only one morph that will get us thousands of kilometres out to sea in the time we have left," he added. "Human."

"Yes!" Rachel thrust a fist in the air. Her face gleamed with pleasure. "Finally. Extreme-Yeerk-butt-kicking!"

I did not express my opinion on the matter.

Cassie spoke again. "Jake. Everyone. Come on. We've gotten this far without totally losing it. By following the rules of basic humanity. No one can deny that."

"I'm not denying it," Marco said coldly. "But Jake's right. Things have changed. We can't be asking any more whether something's right or wrong. We really need to start asking whether it's expedient."

"Whoa." Rachel grinned. "Big word."

You see what I mean by humans being an odd species? Self-contradictory, yet successful. Able to advance their civilization while engaging in continuous ethical debate.

Jake took Cassie's hands in his own. I noticed Tobias turn slightly away.

"Cassie, I'd never ask you to do something you don't want to," Jake said softly. "Or can't. But here's the thing. I think our assumptions are right. I think Visser One is about to launch open war. Entire cities might be incinerated. Whole countries. Maybe, just maybe, if we strike now, if we do everything we possibly can, maybe we can keep that from happening." He smiled sadly. "I'm not sure I could live with myself if we didn't do all that we could."

Billions of lives weighed against the ethics of six "kids". . .

"And I'm not sure I could live with myself if we did," Cassie answered softly. "Jake, there's always a reason to abandon morality. We've been through this so many times. Someone's always saying, 'forget about right or wrong, we've got to win'."

"I know, I know." Jake squeezed Cassie's hands. "But . . . doesn't it always come down to each one of us, all alone, asking ourselves: am I right in doing whatever it takes for the greater good? And, do I trust myself enough to know I won't become evil in the process? It always comes down to something that personal."

Or the situation, I thought. *Or the special circumstances. A morality of convenience. Not unlike Andalite morality. . .*

The thought was troubling.

Cassie smiled. It was not a happy smile, but it seemed to portray a genuine emotion. "If there's one person I trust to keep his decency, it's you, Jake."

Marco folded his arms. Nodded at Rachel. "You, we're not so sure of."

Rachel made a rude gesture with her hand.

A rustling of feathers. <Moving on . . . how exactly do we travel over a thousand kilometres in a few short hours?>

"Easy, Bird-boy. Military jet. Half an hour to the air-force base, maybe a bit more to snag a plane. Then, full speed ahead."

Jake pulled away from Cassie. "OK," he said, clearing his throat. "Let's go."

Chapter 6

"My financial advisor suggested I put at least some money into something safe and slow and steady. The rest is going into something riskier. I mean, my kids aren't going to college for another sixteen years."

"That sounds reasonable. I gotta talk to my accountant though about that ISA plan for my wife. . . What the. . . ?"

Clop-clop. Clop-clop.

I appeared from behind a row of metal lockers.

<Remain calm,> I said.

The male opened his mouth wide. A clear indication he was about to scream.

FWAP!

He slumped to the floor, unconscious. No longer a problem.

The woman, however. . .

"ANDALITE!"

<Yeerk.>

WHAM!

Marco — in gorilla morph — caught her as she crumpled to the ground.

<A little tap on the head never hurt anyone,> he said. <Not much, anyway.>

<Prince Jake, you and the others can demorph now. Marco and I have secured the room.>

One by one, four fleas began to grow and shift into three humans and a hawk.

We were in a locker room belonging to the Air National Guard. Clearly, an organization the Yeerks had succeeded in penetrating.

"Gross." Rachel. "Those pressure suits are hideous."

Jake raised an eyebrow. Not all humans can raise just one at a time.

"Are you saying you'd rather Cassie go in your place? Or maybe that you'd rather explode out of your skin at fifteen thousand metres? Or freeze to death?"

Rachel scowled. Then she bent over the unconscious female Controller.

It had been decided that I would acquire the male.

Also, that I would act as pilot. Without a doubt, I was the one with the most experience of flying aircraft — Andalite, Yeerk and human.

Rachel was to be my co-pilot. I assumed this was because of an attribute Marco calls her "nerves of steel". Rachel would take over as pilot if something should happen to me.

"Come on, people," Jake said. "Let's just get this done."

For a moment, I hesitated.

It isn't that I don't enjoy certain elements of being human. There is taste. There is speech. There is the ability to go to a movie at the multiplex. As long as the running time is less than two hours.

It is just that . . . there is something too compelling about being a human, even for a short time. It makes me uncomfortable.

It makes it seem as if I fit in here.

It is a temptation.

One of the first morphs I acquired on this planet was that of a human male, approximately the same age as my friends.

In order to create that morph, I took DNA from Jake, Rachel, Cassie and Marco — with their permission, of course — and combined it.

So, when I am in this human morph, I am an odd composite of four people, the exact DNA replica of no one in particular.

This is a compromise. A way around the Animorphs' reluctance to acquire and morph other sentient creatures without their permission. And,

29

given the secrecy of our mission, permission cannot freely be requested.

But now. . .

Now, we were committed to doing whatever it took to stop Visser One's aggressive invasion of my adopted home, I was, though not for the first time, acquiring the DNA of a human.

SCHLOOP!

Morphing is a strange and unpredictable process. It never happens in quite the same way twice. And it never fails to be somewhat — disconcerting.

My eye stalks were sucked back into my head. A head that was remoulding to the rounder skull of a human. A head that was sprouting dark-brown human hair.

<Ax, don't you know blonds have more fun?> Marco smirked.

I ignored him.

Concentrated on staying upright as my two front legs dissolved into my broadening chest. Now I was standing on two human legs. I was pleased to discover they were relatively sturdy.

One Andalite heart disappeared into Z-space. The other re-formed to a human heart and began its distinctive beat.

Blue fur faded into skin slightly lighter than Marco's. It was sprinkled with dark, coarse hair in a variety of places. Including the knuckles of my now powerful, five-fingered human hands. I began to attempt to put on the pilot's uniform.

<Marco, come on, man.> Prince Jake, already remorphed to flea.

Marco slammed the door on a locker which now contained the female co-pilot and began to demorph.

Rachel, now in the body of a slightly stocky red-haired woman, secured the pilot — gently — in another locker.

I felt the tiniest tickle on the back of my neck as two fleas jumped on board.

"Ready?" I said.

Captain Felitti's voice was unsteady, betraying my own excitement. My own discomfort.

Rachel grinned. "Let's do it."

Chapter 7

We strode boldly across the airfield.

"Rachel," I said softly, "that is the plane these humans are supposed to take for a test flight."

"What gave it away?" she hissed. "The maintenance crew saluting us?"

"An F-16D, two-seater fighter-bomber. Computer control, I believe. Are you prepared to commandeer the aircraft?" I asked.

"Oh yeah."

We walked swiftly up to the two-person maintenance crew.

Smiled. Saluted.

And then subdued the crew.

"Come on, come on!"

Rachel climbed up into the cockpit's co-pilot seat. I vaulted up into the pilot's place.

The jet's capacity for extreme acceleration required each of us to be in an almost fully reclining position.

Quickly, we strapped and buckled ourselves into restraining belts and harnesses.

Pulled on helmets complete with oxygen masks.

Tested the radio mikes that would allow us to communicate with each other once the jet was off the ground.

I rested my right arm on a special armrest and took hold of the short handgrip that would transmit my orders to the jet's computers.

And without the immediate interference of other Air National Guard personnel or the ground control tower, I started the engines. Taxied. And took off.

It was not very difficult.

"Well, that was lucky," Rachel said. Her voice sounded far away through the microphone though she was not more than several centimetres from me.

"Too lucky. I am afraid the rest of the mission will not go as smoothly."

"Pessimist."

"No. Realist."

We had less than two hours to reach the destination described in the Yeerk transmission.

First: I could not demorph inside the pressure suit without it ripping apart. Which would probably cause my unfortunate and untimely death.

And require Rachel, who could possibly demorph within the confines of her pressure suit, to fly a computer-controlled aircraft at a speed in shocking excess of anything she might have experienced.

Something I was not sure she could do, in spite of her nerves of steel.

At the moment she was grinning. The features of her face were those of Michele Leary. But the maniacal joy was clearly Rachel's.

Second: according to the information we had intercepted from the Yeerks, we were running out of time. There were now less than five hours until the event that would instigate Phase One of Operation 9466.

Suddenly. . .

"*This is Ground Control. Captain Felitti, you took off without clearance and five minutes ahead of schedule. You are off the course set for the test flight. Return immediately to the co-ordinates. We repeat, return to the flight pattern. . .*"

"You nervous, Ax?"

"I have been in less stressful situations," I admitted.

And then. . .

"*This is Ground Control. Whoever you are, return to base immediately. If you do not reverse course you will be shot down. Repeat, you will be shot down."*

Suddenly, on the radar screen — two jets pursuing us.

"Guess they found the real pilots," Rachel said. "And the maintenance team."

No choice.

The F-16D fighter-bomber can reach a maximum speed of approximately two thousand one hundred and sixty kilometres per hour.

Achieving that speed was not necessary.

Yet.

I increased speed to slightly exceed Mach 1.

"Prepare yourself, Rachel."

And shortly, we lost the pursuit planes.

"Woo-hoo! Nice work, Ax. Even though my eyeballs are now stuck to the back of my head."

I checked in with Jake and the others.

The flea morph had protected them from the physical effects of the jet's massive speed.

This seemed to disappoint Marco. Recently, he had claimed to be "bummed" about not being able to ride the new Monster Coaster at The Gardens.

In his words: "What with being officially dead and all now, I'm actually in an F-16D. And I can't feel a thing. My life is great. Isn't my life great?"

We continued to fly. The F-16D handled well for an Earth-built aircraft.

Finally. . .

"Rachel, we are approaching the coordinates. Keep an eye on. . ."

"I see something, Ax!"

"You have a visual?"

"I just said I can see it. It's . . . it's huge. Even I know that's an aircraft carrier."

"I see it. The USS *George Washington*," I read.

"What are those other ships around it?"

"Maybe we should ask Prince Jake."

<The USS *George Washington*.> Marco interrupted. <There's a sick twist on the concept of piracy. The man's namesake aircraft carrier hijacked by Yeerks.>

<We don't know that's what's happening,> Jake said. <Those other ships are part of the carrier battle group, Ax. Probably some destroyers. Some guided-missile cruisers and frigates.>

<Nuclear-attack subs too, right?> Tobias.

<And at least one combat support ship. For supplies.> Marco.

<Cassie,> Rachel said. <Are you feeling a little, I don't know, left out?>

<Yeah.> She laughed. <And somehow it doesn't bother me.>

Chapter 8

"**A**x! Look at the radar. They've spotted us!"

"Yes. I assumed the carrier's surveillance systems are sophisticated enough to spot an air-force-owned F-16D in its airspace."

<Ax, what's going on?> Jake. <Flea "ears" are not, you know, the best.>

<We have been located by the USS *George Washington*,> I told him. <And we were the target of two air-force jets attempting to intercept us.>

<To shoot us down, Jake!> Rachel shouted. <We lost them, but the air force probably contacted the *GW* with a warning.>

<Options?> Jake asked.

<None that I can see,> Rachel said. <Jake, you know the carrier's gonna send some people after us, too. This plane is a liability!>

A split second of silence. Then. . .

<Ax! Get out in front of the carrier. Get in its course and drop the plane. If we make it out of here alive, we'll pick up the ship as it comes by.>

<Maybe if we start demorphing a second or two before impact,> Cassie said, <we'll make it. . .>

<Or not,> Marco said grimly. <Well, I can't say it's been fun. . .>

No choice.

I blocked out the voices of my friends.

Took the plane to maximum speed and concentrated on overtaking the carrier.

And staying ahead of the air-force jets which I assumed would reappear momentarily.

I was being asked to take an enormous risk.

Rachel and I — carrying Prince Jake and the others — could not simply eject.

Because we could not chance being seen and captured in these human morphs. Morphs identical to the two pilots found back at the Air National Guard locker room.

We had to go down with the plane.

But how to "drop" the plane with us on board and survive?

A nosedive would kill us instantaneously.

OK. The plane had to hit on its belly. In effect, I had to perform a controlled crash landing.

The drag undoubtedly would tear the aircraft apart.

But Rachel and I would have some chance of surviving. And with us, our friends.

We were several kilometres ahead of the carrier when I began to cut back our speed.

"Ax, why are you slowing down?!"

"If the plane hits the water at top speed, we will be dead within seconds. If it hits with the engines stalled . . ."

"We'll be dead within seconds!"

I braced myself. The impact would be brutal.

I am the servant of the people. . .

The noise . . . horrifying. . .

I am the servant of my prince. . .

And then. . .

I am the servant of honour. . .

We were down!

The bubble immediately shattered. The jet broke apart.

Cold ocean water roared into the cockpit, swamping Rachel and me.

Blinding me to anything but my own terrible fear.

Desperately, I tried to demorph within the pilot's now-useless pressure suit.

And in my panic, with the powerful rush of water slamming into me, while trying with freezing fingers to unleash myself from belts and harnesses meant to save my life. . .

I began to suffocate!

Andalites do not enjoy confined spaces. Neither do humans when it seems the confinement is about to kill them.

If only my tail would appear, if only the blade would sprout and slice me out of this binding garment. . .

I thrashed. Gasped for air. Swallowed salty water.

Slowly — too slowly! — began to demorph in the cold, dark ocean. . .

Riiip! Slaaash!

Yes!

I was free!

I was Andalite.

I kicked my way to the surface. Scanned madly for my friends amid the wreckage of the jet.

They had been on Joseph Felitti's body. On Michele Leary's body. Where were they now?!

Rachel! Already on her way to seagull.

Clasped under her still-human arm, Tobias was almost fully hawk.

<Prince Jake!>

From a few metres away. . .

"Ax! Nice work. I see Marco."

"Ax-man! The ride of the century!"

"Jake, I'm to your left." Cassie.

We were all alive!

Another too-lucky event.

"Seagulls!" Jake called. "Before some guy up on the island spots us with a pair of binoculars. Then get to the carrier!"

Chapter 9

<This thing is massive,> Cassie said. <It's . . . it's too big to be real.>

<It's a Nimitz class. Biggest warships in the world. Built by Newport News Shipbuilding Company, out of Virginia.>

<Jake?> Rachel cocked the seagull's head. <Do you have a life?>

We had landed, six seagulls, near a radar mast protruding from the island of the USS *George Washington*.

Below us, on the flight deck, approximately thirty planes were parked and tied down.

Marco strutted closer to Rachel. She strutted away.

<Rachel, Rachel, Rachel. There's no such thing as a useless fact. Every tiny, seemingly

42

arcane bit of information our boy Jake spews about aircraft carriers or fighter planes just might be the thing that saves our butts.>

<Marco is correct,> I added. <Prince Jake, what else can you recall regarding this craft?>

<I wasn't expecting to have to recite from memory but ... OK, the first Nimitz class carrier was deployed in 1975.>

If Marco were in his human form, he would have raised his eyebrows at Rachel.

This is how well I have come to know the meanings and uses of human physical gestures.

<Length — about three hundred and twenty eight metres. Overall width, seventy five metres. Area of flight deck — um, one and three quarter hectares. I think.>

<That's my boy,> Marco encouraged. <What else?>

<Speed, thirty-plus knots. That's a little over fifty-five kilometres per hour.>

<More aircraft below,> Marco prompted. <On the hangar deck.>

<Yeah. Eighty-five or ninety, total. I can't remember.>

<Types?>

<Just look down there. A variety. Depends on what the *GW*'s out here for, I guess. Probably some F/A-18C Hornets. E-2C Hawkeyes, maybe some EA-6B Prowlers. F-14D Tomcats. Four catapults for launching. Four aircraft elevators.>

<Crew?> Tobias asked.

<Between five and six thousand, total, full complement. Which is rare these days. Cutbacks.>

<What makes this thing go?> Rachel asked.

Clearly, her interest was piqued. Anything large and capable of aiding in destruction had to be of interest to Rachel.

<Two nuclear reactors. Four main engines. That's geared steam turbines, four shafts. Four propellers. Maybe more stuff, I don't know.>

<Uh-huh.>

<Armament?>

<Generally, the NATO Sea Sparrow missile system. That's two launchers, eight missiles each. I think the *George Washington* has four twenty-millimetre Phalanx CIWS mounts.>

Cassie had been silent until now. <CIWS?>

<Close-In Weapon System. The whole point of the carriers is to provide what's called a "forward presence". They're pretty much the most important part of the picture. In peacetime and during war.>

<Right,> Tobias said.

I suspected this information did not impress Cassie as it impressed the rest of us.

<The humans on board are wearing a variety of uniforms,> I noted.

<That's right.> Tobias. <Navy — sailors and air wing. And marines.>

<What's up with the different-coloured jackets?> Rachel said. <The red ones aren't so bad.>

Jake turned away from the wind. <Flight deck personnel. Different colours for different roles. Jackets are called float coats. You wear the same colour jumper underneath. I'm pretty sure the guys in red are crash and salvage crews. Yeah, and explosive ordnance disposal.>

<No wonder Rachel likes the red,> Marco said.

<What about those in green?> I asked. <Or yellow?>

<It'll come to me. Hmmm. Or maybe it won't,> Jake admitted. <Look, we don't know how this is going to play, but one thing: keep your ears and eyes open. A carrier is a highly organized society. Anyone looking lost or out of place is going to get nailed. No sailors in the aviators' squadron ready rooms and no enlisted personnel hanging around the flag quarters.>

<Which means if any of us goes human, we've got to look and act the part.>

<Right. No calling attention to yourself, Axman. Stay away from the cafeterias.>

<Not a problem,> I replied stiffly.

<And stick with others who are dressed like you,> Jake went on. <You morph a guy who comes with a cranial helmet, you'd pretty much better stick with the other flight deck personnel.>

<But let's try not to morph humans,> Cassie said. <If we can help it.>

<If we can help it,> Jake agreed.

<One thing we should consider,> I noted. <The air force will undoubtedly take responsibility for the crash of one of its jets within sight of the navy's carrier. However, if the Yeerks are already on board, there will be suspicion and heightened security measures. In addition to the possible presence of the air force's own investigative team.>

<So, you're saying this mission is now more dangerous than ever?> Marco asked. Rhetorically.

I answered him anyway. <Yes. I am.>

Chapter 10

<Jake, something's definitely going on.>

Marco directed our attention to a particular area of the flight deck.

Something was going on.

<Looks like preparations for a ceremony or something,> Cassie noted. <Lots of sailors in white uniforms. They look pretty spiffy. . .>

<Maybe an inspection?> Jake wondered. <No. Look. They're getting ready for a landing. Someone's coming on board.>

<And I'm guessing his name is trouble,> Marco shouted over the loud THWOK THWOK THWOK of an approaching transport helicopter.

<Something to do with Operation 9466?> Tobias wondered.

We watched as a perfectly orchestrated *GW* flight deck crew helped the helicopter land.

47

A few moments later, several naval officers emerged from the aircraft.

According to Jake, one of the men was an admiral.

According to Marco, the "big cheese".

And then I saw someone among the admiral's entourage who, in a perfect world, should not have been there. He was wearing a navy officer's uniform like his colleagues.

But I recognized him all the same.

<Prince Jake.>

<I see him, Ax. Chapman.>

<You were right, Marco. The name is most definitely trouble.>

We watched as the captain, the admiral and his entourage went below decks.

Chapman went with them.

<OK,> Jake said. <We're going below. Follow me.>

<Aye aye, Captain. Let's go, me maties!>

<Marco. Please. Shut. Up,> Rachel said, lifting off after Jake.

<You know, I just can't win with her. Tobias, you must be a saint.>

<Cut it out, you two,> Jake said quietly. <Everybody. Do the gull thing. Circle, swoop. Then, one right after the other, drop down the airshaft after me. And keep your eyes open.>

<Oh, goodie. Nothing a bird likes better than to drop down into a narrow, confined space,>

Tobias commented.

I took off after the others. The wind made it somewhat difficult to swoop and glide in the usual effortless seagull manner.

But the men and women on deck had far more important matters with which to be concerned than a few screaming, cawing seagulls being buffeted by powerful ocean breezes.

So no one noticed as, one by one, we dropped down through a sort of chute and on to the deck immediately below. The gallery, or 03 deck.

Once inside the carrier and no longer in the open sky, six seagulls attracted quite a bit of attention.

"Crazy birds! Look out!"

A sailor ducked, covered his head with his arms.

<Follow me!> Jake ordered. <We've got to lose them and demorph!>

The chase was on!

WHOOOSH!

My left wing brushed the side of the narrow, low-ceilinged corridors.

<This is so fun!> Rachel.

<Yeah, you maniac. Crash-and-burn keep away.> Marco.

WHOOOSH!

I struggled to keep aloft. Pumped my wings hard through the artificial environment.

No fresh air. No thermals. No lift!

Down again!

Down a flight of stairs so steep it seemed more like a vertical ladder. No way to fly headfirst.

Feet-first, wings awkwardly held aloft to resist smashing to the ground. . .

<Ow.>

Misjudged the distance between my body and the rapidly approaching floor. Struggled back to my feet. Struggled back into the air. Almost didn't make it. . .

<Down again!> Jake shouted.

Down to the third deck, two decks below the main hangar deck.

Sailors! Behind us, coming at us from all directions, smacking at the air, pounding down the ladders! Alarms shrieking!

"Come on! We've got to get them before they do something stupid like fly into the air-conditioning plant!"

"Or poop all over the place!"

This gave Rachel an idea.

"Ew! Ewewew!"

Fwooosh!

<In here!>

An open door! Maybe a place to land and demorph!

"Shut the door! Lock them in!"

<Out, out, out!>

Clearly the ship's post office was not a safe place for seagulls.

<Jake, buddy, I'm wiped!>

We flapped past emergency diesel generators.

Past a bank of satellite phones.

Unfortunately, a number of personnel were using the phones.

Several of them screamed.

Finally. . .

<The laundry. In here!>

Clumsily the six of us tore into the ship's laundry. The room was very large and hot and steamy.

And, except for one sailor intent upon stuffing dirty clothing into a massive machine at one end of the room, empty.

Prince Jake did not have to tell us what to do.

Chapter 11

We demorphed behind the industrial-sized washing machines.

And then. . .

FWAP!

The sailor on laundry detail would never know what hit him.

Gently, Marco laid him on the floor under a long table and placed a folded sheet beneath his head.

It was decided I would morph the pilot again. A physically fit adult male was a convenient morph for our purposes.

And my own technical knowledge would also be useful.

The others would ride in my pocket as cockroaches. After I borrowed a uniform. The laundry room was obviously the perfect place for that.

"Ah, the glamorous life of a soldier," Marco said, keeping an eye on the door.

<Not so much worse than the lives of some of the crew on board this carrier,> Tobias said. <Guys who work flight deck get hazardous duty pay on top of their regular sea pay.>

<You see, that's what I'm saying,> Marco pressed. <What do we get for risking our butts? Nothing. *Nada*.>

<What about the satisfaction of knowing you're protecting the freedom of all human beings?> Cassie asked.

<Huh. Well, there is that.>

I have become quite an expert on how to wear human clothing. Though I will never understand or like it.

Dressed and with the others in my pocket, I carefully opened the door and stepped back into the narrow corridor.

<OK, Ax, you've got to find Chapman.>

<Yes, Prince Jake>

According to Jake, the aircraft carrier had a crew of close to six thousand. This made my presence less likely to be rapidly discovered — as long as I did nothing to attract attention.

However, the sheer size of the carrier and my relative unfamiliarity with its layout made the chances of my finding Chapman before an evil Yeerk plan unfolded less likely.

I walked. And walked.

The aircraft carrier is a very confusing place. There are many long, narrow, grey-tiled passageways that look identical.

And somewhat dangerous. Along the passageways, at seemingly regular intervals, are raised steel thresholds.

Jake informed me they are called "knee-knockers".

And he warned me to be careful not to trip over them, as that would significantly increase the chance of my being discovered and captured.

I am proud to say I did not trip once.

Another strange thing. Most areas of the carrier admit no natural light. Both sky and sea seem far, far away.

For an Andalite, this is an unacceptable design feature. Especially for a craft on which a person must live for long periods of time.

I walked. Stepped aside to let superior personnel pass, kept my ears tuned to snippets of conversation.

And then . . . bingo. As Marco has been known to say.

"Admiral Carrington . . . the hangar deck. . ."

<Prince Jake? I need to find the hangar deck.>

With Jake's thought-speak directions, I made my way back to the huge hangar deck.

There, I silently joined the crowd of officers gathered around a parked fighter jet. Tried not to call attention to myself.

Hoped the carrier's personnel would assume I was part of Admiral Carrington's staff.

That the admiral's staff would assume I answered directly to the captain of the carrier.

I spotted Chapman at the admiral's side. Chapman. A leader in the Yeerk front organization, The Sharing. Assistant principal at my friends' school. A school Tobias and now Marco no longer attended.

I slipped closer to the admiral. He spoke.

"Captain Plummer, why don't we go to my quarters. There are a few matters I'd like to discuss with you and your senior personnel."

He looked at Chapman and smiled. Turned back to the captain.

"My staff and I have brought back something special to share with you. You know how life in the middle of the ocean can get somewhat, uh, dull."

"Except when the air force dumps one of their jets in your front garden."

There was a ripple of polite laughter in response.

I informed Prince Jake of our new destination.

Marco laughed. <Bet Plummer's hoping for a few bottles of expensive whiskey.>

The crowd of officers thinned to about ten men.

55

Carefully, I followed them back down to the 03 deck, or gallery deck. And to what Jake called the admiral's "flagship", or headquarters.

The officers stopped outside a door. I hesitated. There was no way I could enter without being seen and caught.

<Prince Jake, we need to be inside but. . .>

<Grab two of us and slip us into the captain's pocket, Ax. Stay close. Whoever gets inside, keep communication with Ax and the others.>

I stepped aside. Carefully reached for two of my friends. Slipped them somewhat clumsily into Captain Plummer's trouser pocket.

The captain turned, annoyed.

"I'm sorry, sir," I said. "I stumbled."

And then I hurried off down the corridor.

When it was clear the officers had entered the admiral's quarters, I sidled back up the now deserted, blue-tiled corridor, close to the door.

And listened.

<Ax.> Jake. <Rachel and I are inside.>

Roach senses are weak, far weaker than human senses, for example. But we each have had much experience learning to use the roach's senses to their fullest.

<OK, I sort of hear — ripping? Sounds like the captain's men are opening a box or something. Something large.>

<The admiral was carrying nothing,> I said.

<Maybe someone on the carrier's crew helped set up whatever's going down. . .>

Silence. Then. . .

<Weird.> Rachel. <I'm getting confused. Voices raised, kind of fast. Movement. . .>

<Ax-man! We've got guns drawn! Carrington's a Yeerk!>

<Prince Jake, the gift!>

<Oh, yeah. It's got to be.>

<A portable Yeerk pool.>

Chapter 12

<Ax, we're gonna try to bail, demorph and get firepower before the captain's infested!>

<What should I. . .>

<We're off the captain!> Rachel shouted. <But, oh man, I think they're doing it now. . .>

No choice.

I grabbed Marco, Tobias, and Cassie from my pocket. Placed them at the base of the wall.

<Demorph! Now!>

And in full view of whoever might walk down the corridor, I began to demorph.

Within seconds the narrow gallery deck corridor was impassable.

Stuffed with a heaving, shifting mass of bodies partially human, alien and hawk.

"What the. . ?"

Two crew members, watching from a few metres down the corridor. Mouths open, backs plastered to the wall.

"Oh, great."

Cassie, with the natural grace of an *estreen*, was becoming wolf before I was fully Andalite.

"Please, uh, sirs. Don't panishh. . ."

Then she lost her human voice to the morph.

"Sorry, kids," Marco called to the two sailors. "What my friend was trying to say is that the captain's in a little trouble. Nothing we can't handle. . ."

The sailors tore off down the corridor.

Screeeek! Screeeek!

My tail blade sliced through the metal of the door around the locks.

Marco, now gorilla, threw his weight against the door.

We were in!

From a tiny cupboard on the far wall. . .

A three-hundred-and-fifty-kilo Siberian tiger burst into the room!

In the gloom of the cupboard I could see Rachel rapidly becoming grizzly, able to finish her massive morph now that Jake was gone.

"Andalites!" Chapman cried, turning to the admiral. "Visser Two, get down!"

Admiral Carrington did not get down.

Instead, he threw his arms into the air.

"No Andalite will spoil the glorious mission

59

of the great Visser One and his devoted servant!" he cried.

<That's what you think!>

<Tobias, be careful!>

"Tseeeer!"

One of the admiral's men dropped to the floor, clutching his face, blood streaming through his fingers.

Insanity ensued.

Blam! Blam! Blam!

Eight of the men in naval uniforms were human-Controllers.

It was easy to tell. They were the ones shooting at us.

Two other officers were lying unconscious across a small sofa.

The captain's men, possibly already infested.

Possibly not.

Captain Plummer was sprawled against the table on which sat the portable Yeerk pool.

It was too late for him but. . .

With two hands I grasped the rim of the pool and. . .

SPLAAASH!

Overturned it! Slimy liquid sloshed on to the table and floor.

And in the cascade, two Yeerk slugs.

<Ax, try to pull the fight into the hallway!> Jake ordered privately. <We'll be massacred in here!>

I leaped past the gasping captain and into the corridor.

Looked back to see Jake, a gunshot wound on his back, clamp his jaws around a Controller's wrist.

Shake the gun out of it. Smack the man to the ground.

Saw Rachel lift two other uniformed Controllers like they were dolls.

Saw Marco dodge a bullet that would have destroyed his face. Lunge for the shooter. Take him down.

Maybe we could do it . . . save at least the captain's free men. . .

Isolate Admiral Carrington. Visser Two.

Take him hostage.

Get away before he sent for reinforcements.

Then, flooding the corridor behind me. . .

"Up ahead!"

"What the heck is that?"

Free humans, navy and marines, also armed.

Coming to rescue their captain and admiral.

Coming to kill the crazed animals and blue alien creature who threatened their lives!

It was impossible.

We couldn't protect ourselves.

We couldn't seriously defend ourselves against these men simply doing their duty.

"Aaahhh!"

Cassie had Chapman by the ankle and was

dragging him into the corridor.

<Prince Jake! Reinforcements are on the way. Non-Controllers. We will be slaughtered!>

Jake growled at the Controller who was successfully protecting the angry admiral.

<OK. Everybody! Get out. Now!>

Chapter 13

I ran full out, away from the storming sailors.

Cassie was at my heels.

<In here!> I shouted.

With weak Andalite fingers I grabbed hold of a door handle and pushed.

Together we tore inside. With my back hooves I slammed the door shut.

An office of sorts. Desks, computers, filing cabinets.

One man seated at a console.

Fine. Whatever.

Had to morph. Had to become Joseph Felitti.

"Who are . . . what are. . ."

FWAP!

<Is he OK?>

<Yes, Cassie.> I sighed. <Only stunned.>

Speedily, Cassie demorphed and helped me disrobe the enlisted man.

Cassie has strong convictions. She also is usually willing to help get the job done.

Then I morphed the pilot.

While I dressed in the enlisted man's uniform, Cassie went cockroach.

<What do we do now, Ax? Where do we go?>

I thought. And then it came to me.

The combat information centre.

Jake had mentioned it, told us it was on the same deck as the admiral's quarters.

CIC. The central command and control complex for the aircraft carrier as well as for the entire carrier battle group.

Whatever was going to happen next was likely to happen there. And soon.

<I think I know,> I told Cassie.

And after securing the enlisted man with some available strong tape and a handkerchief as a gag, I stepped out into the corridor.

It was quiet. The Yeerks had restored some semblance of order.

But at regular intervals along the corridor there were now armed guards on high alert. Dressed as navy personnel but undoubtedly Yeerk.

And as I passed two other enlisted men I heard them whisper.

"Bob says he saw a tiger. And LaVerle swears

she saw some weird blue deer. They're being questioned now. I don't know what the heck happened down here. . ."

I did. And I knew what would be happening shortly.

The Yeerks would be making Controllers of the unfortunate witnesses.

I continued to search for my destination, somewhere on this deck.

After ten minutes of purposeful walking, I found it.

The door was closed, guarded by two marines. Without a pass I could not enter.

The door opened and a young navy lieutenant stepped into the corridor. Here was my pass.

<Cassie, I am about to commit another ambush,> I warned the roach in my pocket.

<Do what you have to.>

I followed the lieutenant down the corridor to a tiny bathroom. Knocked him out from behind. Locked the door, demorphed and acquired him. Morphed him.

Dressed in the lieutenant's uniform, Cassie safely in the lieutenant's shirt pocket, I left the bathroom.

<We are about to enter the combat information centre,> I said privately.

The armed guards nodded, stepped aside, and allowed me to enter.

Inside, Admiral Carrington, Visser Two, looking none the worse for the skirmish earlier.

Captain Plummer. Now, a Controller. Perhaps struggling wildly against the slug in his head.

Perhaps not.

And in a corner, watching — Chapman.

The admiral and captain were standing at a screen, watching a flashing blip.

"Sir, we've got what appears to be a Chinese ship-to-ship missile. Fast approaching . . . wait. . ." The technician's voice faded away.

"What else?" the captain barked.

"Sir, another missile, seems to be from the same source. A Chinese sub . . . I think."

Why did the technician sound so puzzled? So disbelieving?

What was happening? And what could I do to stop it?

Three minutes.

Only three minutes until the first time stated in the Z-space intercept.

Something pivotal was about to happen. Phase One of Operation 9466.

But what. . .

Of course.

<Cassie. Who are the Chinese?>

From her hiding place in my shirt pocket, she answered.

<The Chinese? A people. A nation.>

<Are they enemies of the United States?>

<No. Ax, what's going on? The United States has no serious enemies, any more.>

<Well,> I answered, <it is about to.>

BOOM!

The force of the explosion threw me off my feet.

<Ax! What happened?> Cassie cried, panicked.

I stood and steadied myself against a large console.

<We have been hit.>

And all around me. . .

It was all moving too fast!

Everyone speaking at once!

"Prepare flight deck for launch. Catapults number one and two. . ."

". . .air group commander. . ."

"Preparing for launch, sir."

"Bridge indicates. . ."

". . .the ACDS shows. . ."

"Damage report!"

"Several fuel-based fires on the flight deck. They have been contained. Minimal damage to the second and third decks. Below fourth deck, no significant damage."

"Nuclear reactors?"

"Full function."

"Casualties and fatalities?"

"Chief medical officer reporting five men

killed on the flight deck. Casualty report from hangar deck. . ."

<Ax, talk to me!>

<Cassie, we are witnessing an elaborate set-up. The Yeerks have just instigated a world war.>

Chapter 14

<We have to do something!>

<I'm afraid it might be too late. . .>

<Ax! Rachel? Anyone!>

<Prince Jake!>

His thought-speak was dim but understandable.

<Ax, where are you? Are you OK? Who's with you?>

<I am currently in the combat information centre, as are the admiral and captain. Cassie is with me.>

And then I proceeded to tell him what I thought was happening.

That, quite possibly, we were present at the start of World War III.

<Ax-man, I'm nowhere near the CIC. It's up to you. Can you acquire either the admiral or the

69

captain? Reverse the orders to attack. Get the planes and whatever else sent back.>

Impossible!

<I don't see how. Neither is likely to leave this room, certainly not alone. . .>

<Do it, Ax. I know you can find a way. I'll try to establish contact with the others, get us closer to you and Cassie.>

<Prince Jake. . .> But I knew he was now out of range. <Of course.>

I was desperate.

How many of the men and women in that dark and overly air-conditioned room, obeying orders, reading display consoles, assessing damage, communicating with other ships in the battle group, thinking of home. . .

How many of those brave, dutiful soldiers knew they were involved in a diabolical alien scheme to take over the world?

Yes, I was desperate.

Jake had given me a direct order.

And if I did not find a way to execute that order, in a few short hours, the United States and China would be engaged in a nuclear war.

The beginning of a very ugly end.

<Cassie. Be calm. There will be a loud noise. It will be a gunshot.>

<Ax!>

It was a crazy plan, one Marco undoubtedly would call insane.

However, given the flurry of activity and state of high tension that pervaded the combat information centre, there was some chance of its success.

Two marines stood guard inside the room, in addition to those who stood in the corridor. I strode towards the marine who stood to the left of the closed door.

With the force of surprise on my side, I grabbed his arm.

Grabbed his gun. Twisted him around. . .

And shot Admiral Carrington in the leg.

It was only a flesh wound but it served my purpose.

I punched the stunned marine, pretended to wrestle with him for the gun.

"This man shot the admiral!" I cried.

Silently, I apologized to the man I was accusing.

When one is in human morph, it is hard to remember that the human's pain is not your pain. It is hard to remain separate.

Pandemonium!

Within seconds the innocent marine was knocked to the ground by two naval men. In their zeal they also knocked him unconscious. Which was unfortunate for him. But necessary for me.

I watched as two white-jerseyed medics rushed in and knelt by the admiral's side.

"Get off me, you fools!"

"Admiral Carrington, sir, you have to let us help you, sir."

With the skill and expertise of their profession, the medics lifted the protesting admiral on to a collapsible stretcher and hurried him out of the room.

I stepped out of their path.

In the ensuing commotion, no one asked where I was going. Why I was following the medics and their patient to the hospital ward.

"Hold on, Admiral, sir."

In the narrow deserted corridor I began to demorph.

Slipped Cassie out of my pocket. Told her to find the others and get them to the admiral's quarters.

If possible.

And then. . .

FWAP! FWAP!

With a loud thud, thud, the two medics slumped to the floor. The admiral crashed down between their prone bodies.

And before he could shout or struggle to escape — or notice the young girl dashing back the other way — I clapped a hand over his mouth and roughly dragged him into a small room.

"Andalite!" he hissed when I released him. "And I thought Visser One was exaggerating his loathing of you bandits!"

FWAP!

Quickly, I acquired his DNA. Morphed. Dressed myself in his clothes, including the bloody trousers.

Stashed the unconscious bodies of the two medics in a cupboard.

Locked the door behind me and headed back to the combat information centre.

Adrenaline flooded my human body. I fought it down. I had to be cool and convincing.

I opened the door. Stepped inside the room.

"Captain Plummer, recall the planes."

"Admiral?"

I frowned. A popular human expression that can imply seriousness of purpose and/or displeasure.

"I said, recall the planes, Captain. That's an order."

"Sir, with all due respect. . ." The captain glanced down at the dried blood on my thigh. Then to Chapman. "Are you feeling well, sir?"

"Recall. The. Planes. Or, if you prefer, I will relieve you of your command. . ." I looked to Chapman. "And then I will deliver you to Visser One as a traitor."

Chapman's face went white and he nodded to the captain.

"Yes, Admiral, of course."

"I will see you in my quarters," I instructed. "In five minutes."

Everything is going as planned.

Soon you will all be ours . . .

Chapter 15

"What the. . ?"

The captain and Chapman had good reason to be surprised. Because when they reached the admiral's quarters they found not only their visser in his underwear, but an Andalite.

And a tiger. Gorilla. Grizzly. Wolf. And a red-tailed hawk, perched menacingly on a high shelf.

BAM!

The door shut and locked behind them. Rachel plastered herself against it. No way out.

It was up to me to speak. I addressed myself to Visser Two.

<Your plan has failed, Yeerk. At least, the first stage of your plan. The aircraft have been recalled.>

75

The visser smirked. "Well done, Andalite. My, you are a smart bunch. But no matter. Recalling the jets will do nothing to halt the next steps of Operation 9466 being taken."

By this time, I was certain I understood the goal of the visser's plan. But I wanted to hear the horrid scheme from his own mouth.

And we needed details.

<Explain yourself, Yeerk!> I demanded.

Silence, as Visser Two continued to grin.

<Ax, I could just, you know, tear the slug out of this guy's head.>

<Thank you, Rachel. But that won't be necessary.>

To the visser, I said, coldly, <Speak now.>

He sighed dramatically. "I suppose you have waited long and patiently enough for the revelation of my brilliant scheme."

He stood and stuck out his chest. A strange and somewhat pathetic sight, this thin human male posturing in his underwear.

<We got a wacko here,> Marco commented.

"Here's how it plays," the admiral went on. "The non-Yeerk personnel in this carrier group believe we have just been attacked by the Chinese. Which, of course, is a lie. The *GW* retaliated by sending out several aircraft to bomb a genuine Chinese sub — the one supposedly responsible for the attack.

"Kudos. You Andalites have aborted that

phase of the plan. If it had gone forward, that sub would have viewed the American attack as an unprovoked act of aggression. The Chinese commander would have retaliated. Dreadful misunderstanding on top of dreadful misunderstanding."

The visser paused and grinned at his colleagues. I could not help but notice their expressions were somewhat wary.

"However, the brilliant plan proceeds un-hampered! In slightly less than two hours," the visser went on, "no matter what actually happens between now and then, our people in government will receive detailed reports of a vicious Chinese attack on the *George Washington* carrier battle group and order a particular nuclear submarine, manned exclusively by Taxxons, to launch what is by Yeerk standards a quite primitive — however effective — nuclear fusion device against certain Chinese cities.

"The Chinese will respond in kind. War will escalate and spread and, before long, the human population will be severely reduced in number and depleted of weapons. A perfect time for the glorious Visser One to conquer planet Earth!"

<My offer still stands, Ax,> Rachel said.

<Ax, tell him to call off the American sub,> Jake demanded.

<Yeerk,> I said, <if you comply with our

demand we will let you live. If you do not, you will die right here. Contact the American submarine under Yeerk control. Order it to abort its mission. Tell your commander the plan has been cancelled.>

It was a mad and desperate act. Why would this Yeerk comply with the wishes of his sworn enemy?

The visser laughed and sat back in the narrow chair. Crossed one leg over the other and cocked his head.

"And reveal to the mighty Andalites which US submarine is under Yeerk control? Hardly. No, my esteemed foe, I don't fear death. You may kill me now, if it pleases you. The plan will unfold whether I live or die. What I fear is failure."

<Yup, definite wacko.>

Again, Visser Two grinned that disturbing grin.

"The plan proceeds. In approximately two hours, nuclear missiles will fly from an American Trident submarine. Shortly thereafter, the Chinese will respond.

"And how long before all nuclear powers are involved? Russia, France, Great Britain, Israel, India, Pakistan. Equal opportunity destruction. Tens of millions will die. Perhaps hundreds of millions. And the way will be prepared!"

Visser Two stood and saluted to some unseen general power.

<I'm half-expecting to hear him belt out a Yeerk version of that old Nazi standard,> Marco said. <You know, "The Future Belongs to Me".>

<He's insane. A fanatic.>

<Yes, Cassie. I believe that fact has been well established.>

<The question now,> Jake said, his voice betraying his concern, <is how do we negotiate with a psychotic.>

<Negotiate! I say we pulverize— >

KNOCKKNOCKKNOCK.

A voice from the hall.

"Captain! Sir, we have visuals of unidentified aircraft on approach! Dozens, type unknown. And sir, they don't show on the radar scan!"

Instinctively, I raised my tail. Turned my stalk eyes to Jake.

Flinched as wild, high laughter poured from the visser's throat.

"Unidentified, indeed," he cried. "I would rather have done this more cleanly, but one does what one must! Within minutes, my dear enemies, Yeerk Bug fighters and transports will land on the ship. What will you do then, the six of you against the might of the Yeerks? How will you stop me then?!"

I was tiring of rhetorical questions.

Rachel lunged for the man but a harsh word from Jake stopped her.

<No. Everybody, stay calm. We need this

creep. He's the only one who can stop the slaughter from coming down.>

<But. . .>

BA-BOOM!

Anti-aircraft guns!

TSEEEWW! TSEEEWW!

Dracon beams!

<We're under attack!> Rachel cried.

I looked to Jake for direction. . .

And was thrown to my knees as a violent explosion ripped through the admiral's cabin. I covered my head with my arms in a futile attempt to protect against raining sheets of metal.

Through the haze of smoke and crumbled plaster I could see a crouched wolf and a large, dark mass that might have been Marco.

And then the initial impact was over. A sort of silence came upon the cabin.

<Rachel, Ax, everybody!> Jake called.

I stumbled to my hooves.

With four burning eyes scanned the area of destruction.

Saw a bloody Chapman and a smoke-stained captain, separately struggling to their feet.

<Prince Jake,> I said. <The admiral is gone.>

Chapter 16

<L>et's go! Up to the flight deck!>

Jake was right. There was nothing to be done from below decks at this point.

We needed to be at the heart of the battle. To assess the Yeerk forces. To fight.

Jake and Cassie tore up one of the narrow, almost perfectly vertical staircases.

Tobias, a superior flyer, was able to follow.

It was not as easy for Rachel, Marco or me. For one, Rachel could not fit through the opening at the top of the stairs in battle morph.

TSEEW! TSEEW!

Our dilemma was solved by a Dracon beam tearing a hole large enough for the grizzly.

<Thanks. I think.>

<The Yeerks must have seen Jake, Cassie and Tobias,> I said. <Take great care.>

<Actually, I was thinking of painting a big red bullseye on my butt. . .>

Marco was cranky again.

Awkwardly, I followed him to the flight deck.

I will never forget the sight that met my eyes.

The magnificence of the American aircraft carrier. Desecrated by a barrage of Yeerk Dracon fire, yet blasting back in self-defence. Onboard defence systems still in navy hands.

Several noble escort ships, also blazing away at the descending Bug fighters.

And valiant sailors and marines, men and women. . .

Fighting. And dying.

How many were still free? How many already Yeerks?

Through the dense smoke of battle engaged, I could just make out the aircraft returning to the carrier.

<No way they're gonna be able to land!> Marco cried. <They'll be shot down before they have a chance! I'm gonna get to the bridge, see what I can do. . .>

Keeping close down to the non-skid surface of the flight deck, Marco loped off towards the island.

<I will attempt to locate the visser,> I said.

<Good luck, Ax-man.>

Rachel ran towards a Yeerk transport aircraft that was disgorging Hork-Bajir shock troops.

I stepped forward and. . .

BOOOOOOSSSSH! BABOOOOSSSH!

A dreadful series of explosions almost shook me off my feet.

Humans all around me fell to the ground.

No . . . the aircraft I had recalled. Jets. Helicopters.

The S-3B Vikings. The SH-60F/HH-60G Seahawks. Designed for anti-submarine warfare.

Shot down. The wreckage boiling in the water. . .

Marco had not been in time to commandeer the bridge, subdue the Yeerks inside, tell the jets they were flying into an ambush, a trap. . .

"Die, Andalite scum!"

Bam!

Instinctively, I ducked.

And as I did so, swept my tail around in an almost perfect half-circle. One less Controller.

There was no easy way to distinguish one's enemy from one's ally. No easy way to recognize those with a Yeerk in their head. . .

Unless they gave themselves away.

The rather large marine had snuck up behind me. I had seen him coming.

"For the visser!"

FWAP!

I knocked him down the stairwell before he could fire his weapon. His hand, clutching the weapon, followed.

<Ax!>

Suddenly, in Marco's path, a sailor! Armed.

Marco stopped. Stared at the young man.

And then the sailor saluted and ran off towards the bow.

<Whoa. . .> Marco, dark gorilla hair bloodied and burnt, joined me close to the place we'd come up on deck. <Did I just imagine that or are some of the good guys on our side now?>

Yes . . . as incredible as it seemed. . .

<Look. Ahead, by the Yeerk transport craft.>

Members of the US Navy fighting alongside Rachel. Against two-metre-tall Hork-Bajir, the Yeerks' shock troops.

<I suppose the sudden appearance from the sky of large, prehistoric-looking aliens such as the Hork-Bajir makes the presence of wild animals currently native to Earth seem that much more normal.>

<That or Rachel told those guys what she really looks like and promised them all dates.>

<The aircraft, the ones I ordered sent back to the carrier. They were shot down.>

<I know, Ax-man. I'm sorry. I was too late. Besides, the entire bridge is swarming with Hork-Bajir guarding a few Yeerk officers. It would have been suicide even to try to get in.>

<Prince Jake!>

Jake and Cassie, running from the direction

of the stern. Coats matted with blood and darkened with soot.

<This is stupid!> Cassie cried. <I don't know what we're supposed to be doing! All the jets are being destroyed. The Yeerks have taken control of the ship! We saw them on the fantail. . .>

<They've got hold of the Mk. 15 Phalanx,> Jake explained. <And the Mk. 29 Sea Sparrow SAM launchers. Any incoming help for our side is already history.>

<What are you saying?> Marco demanded. <We surrender?>

<No! We haven't lost. But we can't let the visser get away! That's the goal. We've got to find him!>

And then what? I wondered.

But I did not express this thought aloud.

Jake and Cassie bounded off into the smoke.

Marco grunted. <Once more into the fray, Axman. I'm going to help Rachel. See if I can teach some of these sailor dudes about hand-to-hand combat. I think most of them have never actually looked into the eye of the enemy.>

Marco knuckle-walked across the flight deck.

And then I saw him.

Chapman.

Not the visser but someone who could tell me where to find him.

If I asked in just the right way.

Chapter 17

He was dressed as before, in the uniform of a navy officer.

And he was heading away from me. Limping but moving quickly. Almost running.

Running away from the carnage?

Possibly.

No, I thought.

Chapman was one of the worst sort of Yeerks. Eager for glory. Expert at toadying to powerful superiors.

But unwilling to dirty his own hands if he could find someone else to perform the less appealing tasks of invasion.

Chapman was a coward.

I saw him go below decks.

I followed.

At the top of the ladder-like stairs, I halted.

My Andalite body is superior to that of humans in many ways.

However, as recent experience had confirmed, it is not ideally suited for ascending or descending the stairs aboard a human aircraft carrier.

No choice. Time was running out and I had to be mobile.

I took my chances.

Approached a rather tall young man in a purple float coat.

Asked him politely for the temporary use of his genetic material. And his outer layers of clothing.

Fortunately, this young man was one of those who had realized we meant them no harm. Therefore, I was not forced to subdue him.

The young man grinned.

"Dude. I'm honoured. Borrow away. And go get that alien scum."

I acquired another human and immediately began the morph.

Perhaps I should have warned the young man first as to the somewhat disturbing nature of the morphing process.

At one point, just as my face split to form a human mouth, he put his hand over his own mouth and turned away.

Finally, dressed and in possession of a fire-arm loaned to me, I climbed down the ladder.

But where had Chapman gone? Where would he go?

Back to the CIC.

I made my way down to the 03 deck.

Wounded were being carried through the narrow corridors. Sailors — reinforcements for which side? — hurried past.

I kept my two human eyes straight ahead.

Gallery level. The CIC itself would be heavily guarded. Either by the admiral's Yeerks or by the navy's own personnel.

First, I would try the smaller control centres, those operated by various departments. Anti-submarine. Anti-surface.

With some luck. . .

The anti-air control centre. The door was unguarded.

I simply walked right in. Even though under ordinary circumstances a member of the aviation fuels crew would be unlikely to visit.

And there he was. His back to me. Sitting in a chair, drinking what looked like a cup of coffee.

Hiding from the battle.

He was alone in the room.

I shut the door behind me.

I could see his shoulders tense. Then he stood and whirled around.

"You are going to take me to the visser," I said.

Chapman grimaced. "Andalite filth!"

He threw the cup of hot liquid at me.

It was a stupid thing to do.

Swiftly, I removed the weapon from the waistband of my trousers. Pointed it at his heart.

"Tell me where I can find the visser."

I had no intention of shooting a defenceless man in cold blood.

But I am sorry to admit that it was a temptation.

At that moment, alone in a dark room with one of the Yeerks responsible for the atrocities taking place above deck. . .

Alone with one of the Yeerks involved in the launching of a third world war. . .

Alone with one of the Abomination's most ardent supporters. . .

I could barely stand my own rage.

I cocked the trigger.

Panic swept across Chapman's face.

If he gave up Visser Two, Visser One would have him executed.

If he refused, he believed I would put a bullet in his chest.

"Tell me where to find the visser."

Sweat broke out on his brow.

Nervously, he took a step backward.

"Tell. . ."

WHAM!

Chapman screamed.

"Uumph."

And I was thrown forward on to my hands and knees!

The gun skittered wildly across the floor.

Someone had opened the door. Someone had hit me in the back with the door!

I had allowed my anger to get the better of me.

To conquer my awareness of my surroundings.

To cloud my reason!

"Get him! He's an Andalite! Get him!"

I scrambled forward, jumped to my feet.

And turned to find Chapman pointing the gun at me. With him, a Hork-Bajir bodyguard.

The Hork-Bajir stepped forward.

"Wait!" Chapman grinned. "I think I will take you prisoner instead. My own personal prisoner of war. But just to make sure you don't try to break out. . ."

Bam!

I fell to the floor.

Chapman locked the door behind him.

Chapter 18

I ran across a lush field of grass, hooves pounding.

Breathed deeply the good air of the home planet.

Peace. And quiet.

There was my mother, ahead.

And my brother. Elfangor! It had been so long, too long since we had spoken together. . .

"Wha. . ."

I sat up. No lush field. Just the hard floor of the anti-air control centre.

And the blood oozing slowly from my thigh.

Chapman hadn't shot to kill. Just to incapacitate.

How long had I been out? And why had I fainted?

I had sustained far more serious injuries without losing consciousness. Perhaps it was this particular human morph.

Whatever the reason, I was ashamed.

Not only had I failed to gather the necessary information from Chapman regarding Visser Two's whereabouts.

I had also allowed a personal emotion to get the better of my military sense.

This was one episode I would not share with my friends.

Quickly, I demorphed. Becoming Andalite had never felt quite so welcome.

Skreeeeet!

Carefully, I sliced out the lock on the door and broke out of my prison.

The battle itself was now also taking place somewhere below decks. I could hear all too clearly the cries of the wounded. The roar of destruction.

But I was needed at the heart of the action.

Back on the flight deck. Amid the mayhem.

FWAP!

The man was down.

I am rarely, if ever, surprised or sabotaged in my natural Andalite form.

I removed his weapon from his hand.

My tail blade was almost infallible. But I would take no more chances.

Through the narrow corridor I walked.

Past the CIC. Little if any noise from within.

Past the carrier air traffic control centre.

The tactical flag command centre.

A quick check told me that they were empty. As was the joint intelligence centre.

It was likely that most if not all of the carrier's officers were by now either dead or infested.

If any had been lucky enough to have escaped Yeerk clutches, they would be on deck, loyally fighting alongside their people.

Of that I was certain.

I arrived on the flight deck miraculously unmolested.

And immediately spotted Captain Plummer.

He was on the ground. An enormous hole had been blown in his gut.

It was clear he would not live to see the end of this battle.

"Help! You," he cried, signalling to a Hork-Bajir and a human-Controller standing nearby.

I made sure I was unseen.

The human was one of the supposed naval men who had come on board with Admiral Carrington.

The Yeerks looked at the fallen captain. The human's face showed great annoyance.

"Please, help. Take me below decks. I'm one of you!"

"You're nobody," the Controller shouted.

"Your human host has served his purpose. He's dying. Save yourself if you can."

The Controller and the Hork-Bajir walked away.

I approached.

His eyes were beginning to glass over. Still, they showed fear.

<I am not going to hurt you,> I said.

Then I saw the Yeerk struggling out of the man's ear.

I let it happen.

It would not get far.

Awkwardly, I knelt by Captain Plummer's side.

"What have I done," he gasped. "I tried to fight it . . . I tried!"

<No one will blame you,> I assured him.

He looked down in fascination at what had been his stomach.

"I'm dying."

<Yes.>

He reached for one of my hands.

I stayed with him until he was gone.

Chapter 19

Tragedy upon tragedy.

The Yeerks trained Dracon cannon on the other ships in the battle group.

One by one. . .

Horrible explosions!

Towers of smoke and flame, rising what seemed like kilometres into the air!

The destruction was nearly unbelievable.

BUOOOSH!

I jumped out of the path of some sort of incendiary advice, some sort of fireball. . .

Out of the path of the man in flames, stumbling towards me.

No order to this battle!

No plan. No battle lines.

No strategy. No rules of engagement.

Just mad desperation.

Kill or be killed.

Or run away.

Jump into the ocean, be caught in a raging surface fire, be fried to a crisp.

Voices, raised in panic.

Cries for help.

Supplications to personal gods.

Calls for mothers and wives.

Help, help, help. . .

Too many voices!

Ax. Ax. Ax!

I lifted my tail.

"Hey, easy, Ax, it's me. Tobias."

Indeed, it was my friend.

In the body of a navy sailor. Wearing a yellow float coat and jumper.

"The guy's a catapult-and-arresting-gear officer," Tobias explained. "Didn't want to have to do it without his permission. But he passed out when a bird started talking to him so . . . I stashed him out of harm's way. I hope."

<We do what we must,> I said woodenly. <This morph might prove valuable.>

"Yeah. It's letting me look for the visser in places a hawk just can't go. Besides, any flying object around here is getting popped out of the air."

An odd sound through the din of battle.

I swivelled my stalk eyes.

"Some of the carrier's personnel are bailing," Tobias explained. "They're dropping boats into the water like crazy. Don't know how far they're going to get with a sky full of Bug fighters. Maybe if they can make it to one of the other ships. . ."

BOOM! BABOOM!

Tobias and I raced towards the sound of the explosion.

A large, navy-issued life raft, off the port side.

Destroyed. With it, perhaps twenty or thirty humans.

People.

<They didn't even have a chance,> I said.

This navy aircraft carrier, once in devoted service to the people of the United States, had become a floating island of death.

Its captain enslaved and then left to die.

Its crew almost decimated.

I turned away from the scene of wreckage.

Only to witness yet another horror.

A few metres off.

Marco.

Kneeling awkwardly, trying to help a sailor with severe wounds. I could see that from where I was standing. The sailor was dying.

The sailor who had saluted him!

This had to stop.

I had to stop it.

Chapter 20

<Ax!>

Cassie.

Through the smoke she limped towards Tobias and me.

Jake and Rachel were with her. Fatigued, wounded, panting.

I called to Marco.

<We found Visser Two! He's with a couple of Hork-Bajir, just a few metres away. Let's grab Jake.>

"We can take him hostage. . ." Tobias began.

<What difference will that make?> Marco said bitterly. <First off, the Yeerks don't take care of their own. Nobody's gonna come to his rescue by telling us what we want to know. Second: the visser refused to play ball before.

Why should he change his mind now? The Yeerks are winning.>

<Marco's right,> Rachel said, wiping a small stream of blood from her forehead. <The guy's way too focused on the glory. No way he's going to give up the name of that Taxxon-manned sub.>

The visser had refused to "play ball" before.

But Marco was also wrong.

There was one thing that might indeed change the visser's mind.

One thing that might force him to call off the nuclear submarine scheduled to launch an attack on Chinese cities.

Scheduled to kill billions of innocent people.

One thing.

My blood ran cold.

We do what we must.

<Prince Jake,> I said, privately. <May I speak with you alone?>

Jake sent the others to keep watch on Admiral Carrington and his Yeerk.

Now or never. . .

<Time is running out. It is clear that no matter what the consequences to himself, Visser Two will not give up the name or location of the US nuclear submarine. Without that information we cannot act to halt its mission of destruction. And once that mission is accomplished, the rest of the plan will proceed as the visser outlined.

The slaughter will not end until the Yeerks control the planet.>

Jake held his shattered front paw off the ground. Blood pooled between us. <I know, Ax. But what can we do?>

<I have an idea,> I said. <It is a terrible thing I propose.>

A pause. <Go on, Ax.>

<I do not believe Visser Two will be stopped by anything less than the threatened annihilation of his own people. In this situation, here on Earth, the target would be the Yeerk pool.>

I waited. And I felt shame warring with the desire — the need — to win against the Yeerks.

To thwart the conquest of one of my peoples.

The words of the Andalite morning ritual came to me.

The destruction of my enemies, my most solemn vow.

Finally, Jake spoke.

<Ax, I just can't allow that. I can't give the order.>

<Billions of human lives versus ten or twenty thousand,> I said.

He had to see. Had to be made to see it was the only way.

I continued, <Many of whom are unwilling slaves. Many of whom would welcome death for the sake of freedom.>

<No, Ax, I can't. You can't. What are you

saying? Do you know what it will do to us?>

And at that moment, hearing the shock and horror in my prince's voice, I knew I had made a dreadful mistake.

I never, ever should have laid such a burden on my friend. My ally.

Never, ever should have asked a human of such superior quality to make a decision that would undoubtedly risk the lives of everyone he had ever known.

That would undoubtedly destroy his home, his neighbourhood, his city.

That would utterly decimate his every precious bond to sanity.

I was an Andalite.

A member of the species some unkindly but perhaps rightly have called the meddlers of the galaxy.

I was an alien.

I would carry the burden.

<I am sorry, Prince Jake,> I murmured. And then I hit him alongside his head with the flat of my tail blade. <So very sorry.>

Chapter 21

<Cassie! Prince Jake is unconscious, on the far side of the island. I suggest you go to him at once.>

<I'm on it.>

A wolf leaped from its observation post behind an overturned wrecking crane.

Trusting me.

Never doubting I had Jake's best interests at heart.

Never assuming I could be, technically speaking, a traitor.

I waded further through the burning wreckage and across the deck littered with fallen men and women.

Wounded and dead.

Controllers and free humans.

The awful sound of the dying bruised my hearts.

The scream of Dracon fire and pistols, failing engines and crashing waves pierced my ears.

I spotted my three remaining comrades, not far from where Cassie had been watching.

Crouched in and around a shattered forklift and the burned skeleton of a tractor.

Within view, in the area I later discovered was called the "Hummer Hole", was Visser Two.

He was standing next to the remains of an E-2C Hawkeye. Gesturing wildly to his Yeerk companions. His face a mask of crazed triumph.

<Rachel, Marco.>

<What's up, Ax-man?>

I focused all four eyes on my fellow Animorphs.

<I need your help. I must commandeer a plane. And the visser must be inside when I take off.>

Rachel laughed. <What? Cool.>

<As far as I can tell,> I continued, <there is only one jet not destroyed or chained down. It is already in place at the number one catapult. I believe it is an F-14D Tomcat fighter-bomber. Tobias?>

I turned to the adult male catapult-and-arresting-gear officer Tobias had morphed.

<You must get me two pressure suits. Then you must get to the catapult control pod and

launch the plane as soon as I am in the pilot's seat and give the command.>

"Ax, are you out of your mind?"

Tseeew!

"Aaaahh!"

A naval officer dropped and rolled. Got to his knees and returned the Hork-Bajir's fire.

In the distance someone was firing the Mk.15 Phalanx's Gatling gun.

If anything, the fighting had intensified.

<What's going on, Ax-man?> Marco shouted. <Where's Jake?>

I was prepared for Marco's suspicions.

<Prince Jake is injured. He is temporarily out of commission. I am doing what I must.>

<What's wrong with you, Marco?> Rachel yelled. <Things are bad. Let's go get the visser.>

"Yeah," Tobias cried. "It's a crazy plan, but there's no time, man!"

<Tobias — have either of you wondered what's going to happen after Ax gets the plane in the air?>

Neither Tobias nor Rachel answered.

Marco turned and stared hard at me.

<You Andalites. You people have a tendency to destroy what you want to preserve. And that plane is carrying a nuke. I saw it being fitted up by some of the visser's men.>

<Oh, my God, Ax. . .>

That was perhaps the one and only time I

have ever seen Rachel stunned, shocked.

<You're not acting under Jake's command,> Tobias said neutrally. As if reinforcing the fact for himself.

I knew Tobias well enough to know he would act on his own conscience.

I also knew there was no time for subtle argument or soul-searching.

I needed their help.

Now.

<Marco, I have not always trusted you. But you have always proved me wrong. You have always acted for the good of the mission. Put all personal concerns aside in order to win. To defeat the Yeerks. You have even sacrificed your life as a normal human youth. Please — trust me to do the same.>

Marco laughed harshly.

<Oh, I trust you to be ruthless, Ax-man. Ultrafocused. Heartless, even. What I'm not sure of is what this stunt is all about. Is it really about saving human lives? Or about pumping up Andalite glory?>

His remark stung.

But I had expected as much.

<Please,> I said. <This war cannot come to pass.>

Marco hissed a word I have been told should not be uttered in polite company. Or the presence of parents and teachers.

105

Tobias put a hand on my arm.

<Do you have even the smallest idea of what this will do to your head, Ax-man? Whether you win or lose?>

They had to be made to listen. To understand.

Time was running out.

It was now or never.

I would accept the consequences of my actions.

I would accept full responsibility.

I was the alien.

<Will you help?> I pressed. <For your people. Rachel?>

She looked to Marco as if for guidance.

Tobias looked away.

Marco looked back to me. <We say there's always a choice. Is there, really? Let's go.>

Chapter 22

<Out of my way, jerk!>

That would be Rachel, tossing aside a Hork-Bajir soldier guarding the F-14D Tomcat with the ease of a cat playing with a mouse.

Then, another.

Fwap!

I eliminated the final guard.

And under cover of the body of the jet, I morphed the pilot.

Stepped into my pressure suit and other necessary gear.

Then I climbed inside the plane using its retractable boarding ladder. Made note of my surroundings.

A large canopy. Three rear-view mirrors.

Good. Three hundred and sixty degree visibility, or close to it.

Somewhat old-fashioned control panels, with traditional dial gauges. Primitive by Andalite standards.

Control stick and throttles, all covered with buttons.

I surmised this design feature allowed the pilot to keep his eyes on the sky and still perform his other duties.

And behind me, the radar intercept officer's seat. No flight controls. Good.

<Coming through!>

Marco, wearing a new gash across his massive chest. Carrying a struggling Visser Two under his left arm.

<I would have been here sooner,> Marco said, <but the visser's buddies didn't want to let him come out and play with me.>

"Andalite scum! Put me down this instant!"

<Sorry, guy. But you're going for a little ride,> Rachel replied.

"It doesn't matter what you do to me! I willingly sacrifice my life for the goal of Yeerk domination!"

<Yeah, yeah,> Marco muttered. <We heard you already.>

<Really. He's getting seriously boring.>

Together, Rachel and Marco stuffed the visser into the second pressure suit and helmet. Then they heaved the raging Yeerk into the RIO's seat behind me.

With my dexterous human fingers, I tied his hands behind his back, bound his ankles together. Then I strapped him in.

A dead Yeerk was of no use to me.

Neither was one who would attempt a murder in flight.

I needed him to talk.

<Is Tobias in place?> I asked as I strapped myself in.

I watched Visser Two settle into angry silence. His eyes glittered with what I recognized as rage. And possibly dementia.

<Tobias?> I called in private thought-speak.

I imagined my good friend in his stolen yellow jacket and jumper. At the catapult control pod beneath the flight deck.

Under ordinary circumstances, a civilian would never have been able to infiltrate such a place.

Would never have been able to impersonate such an important person as the "shooter".

These circumstances were very far from ordinary.

<Ready, Ax.>

I knew that what I was about to do was insane.

And that, more immediately, given our in-experience with the catapult-launching system, the launch itself would be extremely dangerous.

It was quite possible the plane would be thrown into the ocean. Or worse.

Marco acted as plane handler. Directed me forward on the catapult. Checked that the "holdback" was in place.

Then he looked up at me, doubt in his gorilla eyes.

Or perhaps the expression can be more accurately described as disbelief.

Then he gave me "the thumbs-up".

Then he turned away.

<Be careful, Ax.> Rachel laughed, but I did not imagine the fear in her voice. <Don't do anything I wouldn't do.>

<Ax! Stop!>

Prince Jake. Running towards the jet. Cassie bounding at his side.

My human eyes began to tear. I widened them, then blinked rapidly to clear my vision.

Ignored the now muttering Yeerk.

<Pressure's where it should be, Ax! I think.>

<Thank you, Tobias.>

I selected the engine setting: afterburner.

<You may hit the button.>

And then. . .

The holdback snapped and the aircraft was thrown down the catapult track!

Unbelievable!

We were hit with several times the force of gravity!

I struggled to breathe.

I felt the very skin of my borrowed human

face stretch towards the back of my head.

My cheeks seemed to spread like putty. My eyes to burrow deep within my skull.

I thought I would die.

At the very least, be unable to take control of the plane.

The roar was deafening. . .

And then the towbar popped out of the shuttle and the plane, having reached flying speed, was on its own.

I was on my own.

Chapter 23

I took the jet back towards the coastline.

Luck was with me. We were not pursued by Bug fighters. Clearly, it was thought the pilot of the aircraft was on an official, Yeerk-authorized mission.

"What are you doing, Andalite?"

I kept my eyes focused on the instrument panel, on the radar screens. I was glad I could not see my passenger's face.

"This plane carries a nuclear device, Yeerk," I said. "As you well know. Primitive by Andalite standards, perhaps even by Yeerk. But effective nonetheless. The bomb is set to explode on impact."

I paused. Relished the tension my hesitation was creating in the visser. Loathed myself for playing this sort of shameful game.

For inflicting a kind of torture.

"That impact," I continued, slowly, calmly, "will occur directly over the Yeerk pool. You may launch World War III on planet Earth, Visser, but how many Yeerks will be alive to benefit?"

"Never!" The man's voice was like the panicked screech of a wounded animal. "Never! You'll never do it!"

I did not answer him.

There was not much time before the scheduled attack by the Yeerk-manned American submarine.

I continued to increase speed.

As I did so, the F-14D's wings automatically reconfigured. Swept back to reduce drag.

I noted this feature with pleasure.

"You won't have the nerve to do it, Andalite!"

Still, I remained silent.

And flew the twin-engined fighter closer and closer to land.

The sky was slowly darkening. It was early evening.

All over the United States — in each and every time zone — millions of humans were going about their daily lives.

Oblivious to the enormous threat to their way of life. The enormous threat posed by the Yeerks and another world war.

Oblivious to the only slightly less enormous

but much more immediate threat faced by a smaller number of Americans.

Ten to twenty thousand human beings faced imminent annihilation.

Annihilation that would be instigated by me.

Fingers tingling, I armed the bomb.

No going back. I had committed to this insanity.

"You're out of your mind!"

I heard the man twisting violently in his seat, desperate to free himself.

Finally, I spoke.

"It is very simple, Yeerk. Contact your submarine. Order the commander to self-destruct. Or I will annihilate the Yeerk pool."

"You'll kill tens of thousands of humans! Non-Controllers as well as Yeerks!"

The jet streaked towards the Yeerk pool.

Closer, closer.

Sweat trickled down my brow and from under my arms.

I felt my human heart almost breaking through my chest.

The sadness threatened to kill me.

Closer. So close.

"Yes," I said. "I will."

And then . . . a miracle.

"All right! You win, Andalite." The visser spat again before going on. "I will order the submarine to self-destruct. But on your honour, Andalite," he cried, "on your so-called honour, you will release me!"

I do not know if I have ever felt more exhausted, more drained than I did at that moment.

I reduced speed. Noted the aircraft's wings sweep forward.

Turned on radio communications.

"You may use the radio now, Visser Two."

I listened as the Yeerk angrily gave his order.

For now, we had won.

I steered a course over the woods I have called home ever since being rescued by Prince Jake and the others.

I was glad to be going back there tonight.

I was also afraid of what I would find. Because "home" meant more to me than just my scoop and the surrounding landscape.

Home meant my fellow warriors. All of them. And I had risked my relationship with them, especially with my prince, by doing what I had done.

It had been a terrible long shot. As Cassie might say, I had played God. And what right did I — an Andalite — have to do that?

I had chanced the lives of thousands of humans for the sake of millions.

And in doing so, I had acted as had many Andalite warriors before me.

I had presumed. I had meddled.

115

I had acted as I had often condemned.

And I had won — we had won — but at what personal price?

Would my friends ever forgive me?

Would I ever forgive myself?

"Would you have done it, Andalite?" The visser's angry voice broke into my solemn thoughts. "Would you really have done it?"

I was unable to respond.

I have enough to answer for.

An awful silence followed Toby's words.

This was bad.

Capture is the stuff of nightmares, something we all fear. Unless you immediately escape or die, it means the betrayal of everyone you love and everything you value.

Because a prisoner is infested by a Yeerk. His brain is probed. Every useful memory, all relevant knowledge, is extracted and stolen for the Yeerks to use.

The Yeerk with access to the once-free Hork-Bajir's mind would have the knowledge to lead an army to the valley. Yeah, the Ellimist made it strangely difficult to locate the valley. But with a guide, the Yeerks would absolutely find their way.

"It's a no-brainer." Marco. "Haul butt before the Yeerks attack."

"There's no other way," Cassie agreed. "Even with our help, Toby, you can't fight an army of Yeerks. They have sophisticated weapons. Lots of reinforcements. There are fewer than a hundred of you." Cassie gestured to the crowd of Hork-Bajir. "Not more than sixty of you who are fit enough and old enough to fight."

"It's not fair," Rachel said angrily.

<No,> Tobias agreed. <But what choice is there?>

Toby was silent. Her expression showed nothing. She turned to Ax.

"The forest is too thick for the effective use of Bug fighters, isn't it?" she asked. "And the valley's too narrow."

Ax's stalk eyes scanned the closely spaced trees. <That is true. But that fact only improves the odds by a very small percentage.>

Toby turned to me now. "Will you help us defend our valley, Jake? Our home?"

I was getting a little annoyed. Toby didn't seem to get it. If we tried to fight the Yeerks, we'd be slaughtered.

"We want to help," I said. "But not if it means setting you up to lose."

Toby looked up into the trees, then turned to survey the camp. She planted the stick she was holding into the yielding ground.

"This valley is our home," she said loudly. "We will not give it up. We'll stay and fight."

Marco threw his hands up in exasperation. "Let me understand what I'm hearing here. You all want to die, is that it?" He looked around at the other Hork-Bajir who remained politely withdrawn from our discussion. "Don't be insane! Mum, Dad? You're with them?"

Marco's parents were as diffident as the Hork-Bajir. They stood impassive and expressionless, feet firmly planted on the hard-packed dirt.

I rubbed my forehead and tried to think. Time was running out. The Yeerks were probably already on the way. Preparations had to be made.

I climbed into the V of a nearby tree, up about three metres so everybody in the camp could see and hear me.

"Listen," I shouted. "The Yeerks will probably be here by tomorrow morning, at the latest. They will kill or infest all of you if you don't leave right now. Everyone must prepare to move out. We'll help you find a new camp."

No one moved.

"Jake," Toby said. "No Yeerk will drive us from this home. I am willing to stay and fight and so are my people."

Grunts of accord rose from the free Hork-Bajir.

I couldn't believe what I was hearing.

"Wait!" I yelled. "You know the Yeerks have advanced weapons. You've seen the Dracon beams. Save yourselves!" I looked at Toby. "Escape now. Live to fight another day!"

No one answered.

Marco strode angrily towards his parents, like he was about to give them a piece of his mind. Rachel glanced up at me with her trademark fearless look. She wanted me to reconsider.

Fine, we were taking sides. The decision would come down to a vote. I jumped from the tree.

"Come on!" I shouted, desperation pounding in my brain. "All those who want to live, stand over here with me. Those who want to die at the hands of the Yeerks, stand over there, with Toby."

There was no mumbling, no movement.

<This is your decision,> Tobias said to the Hork-Bajir. <But I think you should listen to Jake. He only wants what's best.>

"We all do," Cassie said.

I glanced at Ax. He stood a bit apart, aloof. He wasn't giving his opinion.

A serious question for Andalites, especially now for Ax. Meddle where you might not belong. Possibly save lives in the process. Or just walk away. Let a people decide its own fate.

A young Hork-Bajir stepped out from the crowd and walked towards Toby. He stood straight and tall at her side. Jara Hamee and Ket Helpek joined him. Others followed.

Until every Hork-Bajir in the colony stood with their leader.

ISAIAH FITZHENRY

I threw back the flap of the hospital tent and entered. Light became darkness. Cool, fresh air became a stifling, acrid stench.

The smell of sickness and death.

I moved forward, eyes straining to see.

"Ah!"

I bumped into something warm and soft and drew back instantly as the object voiced a high-pitched objection.

"I beg your pardon!" I groped to find a tent pole. "Sally, is that you?"

As my eyes adjusted, I saw a woman standing over a table, wringing out a bloodstained cloth into a bowl of water.

" 'Tis I, Lieutenant," Sally answered with more cheerfulness than I expected. "You'd be looking for the prisoner?"

"That I would, Sally." Sally Miller is a woman from town. If Sinkler's Ridge is worth its place on the map, it is thanks to her. We'd have lost more men by now were it not for the morale boost the men found in Sally's excellent care.

"This way," she said. "We sectioned him off

so he wouldn't upset the others. He's restrained, of course, but I saw to his wound."

"You're a wonder, Sally."

"So my husband tells me on occasion. But these men need me, Lieutenant, and I believe in their cause." She pulled back a pitifully soiled sheet strung up between the tent wall and a post. "The Union cause," she emphasized, turning to leave me with the Confederate soldier who lay on the floor.

His wrists and ankles were bound. The fresh white bandage wound round the left biceps had just begun to soak through with blood.

He stared at me with defiant eyes.

"So the Union has a kid in charge," he said softly. "Yankees got a boy commander."

The derisive remark cut through my pride and struck anger. I was fully aware that I didn't look the part. I didn't need reminding.

"And yet," I answered, "my men have managed to shoot and capture you. That's not bad for child's play."

"I cut you off," he said to console himself. "With no telegraph, Yank, you're as forgotten as on a desert island. Only difference here is that you're about to take a pounding."

"Is that right?" I mocked, intentionally disbelieving.

"Darn right!" he raged. "General Forrest has five hundred troopers in Springville, plus a reserve of—"

He stopped short.

His eyes grew wide as he realized what he had done.

I now knew what the enemy's approach would likely be, their number and their position.

"I thank you, sir," I said, bowing my head. "You have been very helpful."

He kicked the air and lunged as if to strike me, but the pain in his upper arm would not allow it. He fell back in a heap, cursing, sweating.

And I forgot my anger long enough to empathize.

This low-ranking Rebel was fighting for a cause he thought was right. For his home, his people.

He was badly mistaken.

But that didn't change his valiant spirit. Were our roles reversed, I hope I would rally in kind.

I returned the soiled sheet to its position.

"You'll be wanting to visit your own men now?" Sally asked, pointing at a canvas flap beyond which lay my men.

No, I didn't want to see them. I didn't want to see suffering I could do nothing about.

I hesitated.

"It would be good for morale," Sally urged. "And your friend, Corporal Carson, has been enquiring after you."

"Yes, of course," I said. I ducked through the canvas before I thought better of it.

The bodies of my detachment lay motionless, packed tight in the tent like sleeping sardines.

I walked down the narrow aisle, looking in vain for signs of recovery.

"Isaiah," a slender voice called from knee-level.

Mac Carson's half-open eyes looked up into mine. Corporal Carson. We'd grown up together, been schooled together and now fought side by side. Despite the new scar on his left cheek, he looked like the boy I'd always known. Big bones, white teeth, black hair, green eyes.

I knelt and placed my hand against his forehead. It was on fire.

"What news?" he whispered.

"Twenty-five men," I said flatly. "That's all we have. Forrest's force may be over five hundred."

Mac wheezed.

"Thirty men came down from the hills this morning," I continued. "They want to fight."

"Thank God," Mac said firmly. His family was progressive on all counts, abolitionism among them. "You need the men and they've a right to fight. It's their war, too, now."

"Be rational, Mac! You sound like the little man who leads them."

"Jacob?"

"How did you know of him?" I asked, astonished.

"I met him when we came into town. He came down alone, looking for work. We shared some soft bread."

"You spoke to him?"

"I should say! He's quite educated," Mac said. "Taught himself to read and write, but hid it from his former master who would have sold him South to be sure. He never knew his mother or father. They were sold or traded or some such abominable thing."

"Has he been whipped?"

"I imagine so, though probably not often. I've sometimes thought that living life under the threat of whipping and punishment would be just as bad as the thing itself. Perhaps worse."

"I suppose," I said absently, glancing around at my lifeless men. I was almost certain that the body next to Mac had ceased to breathe.

"Can you cover my feet?" Mac asked.

I moved to the end of his cot and nearly gasped. The first two toes on either foot were bloody and brown.

"Frostbite," he said with a weak smile.

I wrapped the wool blanket around them.

"Raines doesn't think we'll be able to hold off the enemy," I said.

Mac coughed and nodded.

"Let the Negroes fight," he said.

I rose to my feet in frustration.

"Isaiah," Mac said, catching my arm. "They're our only hope."

JAKE

"They're going to fight with or without us," Cassie said, awed. As if maybe she'd suddenly changed her mind about what our role should be. "They're risking everything for their freedom."

"We have to respect that," Rachel said. "And we owe it to the Hork-Bajir to help."

I still couldn't believe what had just happened.

<This is just plain amazing,> Tobias said to us privately. <These Hork-Bajir know who they are and what they want.>

"OK." I sighed. "We'll help you."

Marco glanced at me with a mix of exasperation and resignation. He knew this was an argument we couldn't win.

Cassie flashed me a look that said I'd done the right thing.

Toby smiled the strangely frightening Hork-Bajir smile.

"Tobias, as always, you're our eye in the sky. Check out the area and see if you can spot an escape route. I have a feeling we're gonna need one. Marco, get in touch with Erek. See if a few Chee can cover back home for those of us who need it."

Toby stared at me.

"If we need to escape," I corrected myself and smiled.

I began to draw a rough map of the area in the ground with a stick. Toby walked over to where I was crouched down.

"Thank you," she said.

"Yeah, well . . . I just hope your people understand what they're getting into. It ain't gonna be pretty."

"They understand much more than you give them credit for, Jake. They've been called upon to defend themselves before. They've been through a lot."

I nodded sheepishly and looked back at the earth map.

After a while, I ventured further into the camp to check on the battle preparations. With advice from Rachel and Ax, the Hork-Bajir were positioning platforms in the trees.

A Hork-Bajir with a bundle of small branches on his back and a coil of rope in his hand would scramble up a trunk, using heel and wrist blades to climb. Like a telephone repairman in fast forward. When he'd get about ten metres up, he'd dig his ankle blades in firmly, lock in with both knee blades and lean back. With both hands free, he'd lash the branches together. In about ten minutes, there was an elaborate but perfectly camouflaged platform.

When the builder finished, he'd climb on to

the platform to test its strength. Then he'd descend quickly, move to another tree and begin again.

Younger Hork-Bajir then climbed to the completed platforms and stocked them with spears and arrows. Weapons the female Hork-Bajir were turning out with speed, efficiency and skill. It was unbelievable to watch.

Hork-Bajir elders, the few who weren't quite as quick at climbing as they used to be, dug pits and trenches all over the camp. After one was dug, the very smallest Hork-Bajir children were lowered into it to place pointed wooden spikes into the earth. Whoever fell into these holes would come out looking like Swiss cheese. If they came out at all. With the spikes in place, the kids were hauled up to help cover the pits. First with twigs that spanned the opening. Then with leaves that formed a bed to conceal it completely.

Satisfied as I could be under the circumstances, I called the others and Toby to the map to discuss strategy.

"We're here." I pointed to two long, parallel lines marking the narrow passage. "On either side of us are steep banks and cliffs. Impossible to climb without serious time and effort. So I think the Yeerks will come up the valley this way," I said, pointing. "From the south, uphill."

"That's good for us," Marco said.

<It will slow their approach,> Ax agreed, <but it will also interfere with our retreat. Tobias said our only escape route will be up the valley to the north.> Ax pointed to a place where the valley widened, about two kilometres north of the camp. <The valley walls become easier to climb at this point, but will still be slow and difficult.>

I looked at Toby.

"You'd be much better off climbing the valley walls now and fighting from up there."

"We will defend our home."

<We've got another problem,> Tobias said. <I spotted a group of campers. And they're going to be in the Yeerks' way.>

"I guess we'll have to try to convince them to get out of there," I said.

Cassie put her hand on Toby's arm. "Even if you survive, you'll have to go into hiding. Where will you go?"

"If we're forced to withdraw temporarily," Toby said calmly, "we'll go to the hills."

"But the trees in the hills aren't the same kind as the ones in the valley. And they won't provide great shelter. You'll have to adapt all over again."

<And those hills are getting pretty close to the suburbs,> Tobias added. <It wouldn't be safe to stay there very long. Eventually, you'd run into some humans.>

"Maybe it's time the Hork-Bajir did run into

some humans," Rachel said. "We can't count on the Ellimist to appear and help out just because we want him to. If the right people knew what was going on, all sort of things could happen — good and bad.

Marco smirked. "News flash: your average suburbanite ain't gonna tolerate a two-metre-tall bladed alien for a neighbour. I mean, car sharing? Toby as a football mum? Think about it."

Toby's eyes dropped.

"I'm sorry. We don't think of you as freaks, but the average guy on the street? Toby, humans can't even deal with other humans who support a rival football team."

"Yes," Toby said slowly. "I've learned that humans don't care for groups unlike their own."

"That's not always true," I said.

<My study of human history suggests that Marco and Toby are both correct,> Ax said carefully. <Historically, humans are among the least tolerant species in the galaxy, set apart by the prevalence of violence and oppression."

"So, what would you suggest, Ax?" Cassie asked. "Send the Hork-Bajir to a distant planet? All because humans are tolerance-challenged? That can't be the only answer."

"It stinks," Marco said. "But take a look at what humans have done to animals. If there's a chance to dominate, we grab it. I'd rather be a tiger or elephant on Neptune than a striped rug or an ivory box on Earth. The further away you can get, Toby, the better off you'll be."

For a moment, Toby said nothing.

"But are we really that different from you?" she said finally.

She turned towards camp. Towards a Hork-Bajir who bent low to the ground and scooped her crying child into her arms.

The child had fallen. The mother carefully raised the child to her shoulder and gently patted its back.

No, the Hork-Bajir weren't really that different at all.

ISAIAH FITZHENRY

At sundown, Sergeant Raines and two other soldiers walked with me down the main street of Sinkler's Ridge.

Sally Miller and her husband, Joe, were hosting a Christmas party. They'd been kind enough to invite us and we were happy to oblige.

I detailed a number of men for picket duty and left Sergeant Spears in command until our return. Our pickets were spread out through the woods and hills skirting the town. Before the enemy attacked, we would be alerted.

Several townsmen, Joe Miller among them, brought their own shovels and picks and joined us in the digging this afternoon. They wouldn't work near the black men, nor even within sight of them. They said Jacob's men were a disgrace to the Union.

Perhaps. But no one can deny the progress they made. Trees covering the entire south face of Topper Hill were felled and left lying, a formidable defence when time is short.

And the Negroes shaped the earthworks like seasoned engineers. Most of the men dug all afternoon, and would dig all day tomorrow.

We stopped before a white clapboard house with candles flickering warmly in the windows. Fiddle music filtered through the walls and under the door. I climbed the stairs and let the knocker fall.

Scents of cinnamon and vanilla rushed out as the door opened. Sally greeted us warmly. "Lieutenant. Hello, Raines. Welcome."

Sally was resplendent with golden hair bouncing in ringlets and a red-trimmed dress to match her lips. She stepped back to let us enter and nodded as we passed.

We were drawn in by the sound of music and voices. Raines hastened to the banjo case that stood in the corner, threw it open and pulled out the instrument like a child opening a gift on Christmas morning.

Private Tweed raised a tambourine. Corporal Fox unsheathed a pair of bones from his jacket pocket. No words were exchanged. They simply joined the town fiddler, then started in on a new song, the words of which I'd heard before.

"I hear the bugle sound the calls
for reveille and drill,
for water, stable and tattoo,
for taps — and all was still.
I hear it sound the Sick-Call grim,
and see the men in line,
with faces wry as they drink down
their whiskey and quinine."

The stress of the impending attack seemed to melt away. The townspeople present clapped and tapped their feet in time. The young tin whistler and drummer boy, the two I'd seen out my draughty window, watched from beside the roaring fire.

"Good evening, Lieutenant," Joe Miller said. "Merry Christmas." He was a broad man, built for agricultural life. His beard and moustache were even redder than his hair. His wide smile matched his frame.

"And to you, Miller," I answered. "As you see, my men are glad to put aside their duties."

"Come." Miller took me by the arm and led me to a long table by the window. "Sample the foods my Sally has prepared."

My mouth dropped open at the sight.

Spread across the table were the foods I dreamed of at night. Milk, cheese, cake, preserves, boiled ham, turkey, pudding, pickles and loaves of fresh-baked soft bread.

"Eat up," Miller said. "Maintain the strength you need to save this town."

I reached for a buttery cinnamon roll.

"I wish that I alone could save it," I said solemnly. "As you know, our ranks are thin. We may need to arm the men that came into camp today. They're willing to fight, and they—"

"Are you mad?!" The joviality drained from Miller's face. He bellowed as though addressing a plough horse.

"I assure you I am not," I said quietly.

Raines appeared beside me at the buffet table. The song had finished. The guests were clapping loudly.

Miller appealed to Raines.

"Your lieutenant says he would arm a band of runaway Negroes and let them fight the Rebels," Miller said, forcing unwilling laughter from his throat and patting Raines on the back. "Is he a jokester, Raines? Or does he take to the bottle in the evening?"

"I assure you, sir," I said, loudly enough to silence some of the guests. "There is no joke intended, nor any drunkenness among the detachment."

Miller's face grew still, like a bull before the charge.

"Once you arm those Negroes, what stops

them from running wild?"

"Have you met the men, sir?" I said.

"I wouldn't go within fifty feet of those people. I don't need to meet a wolf to know he'll cause all kinds of mischief. They'll take our chickens, our pigs, the house!"

"The Rebels will do far worse if they take the town. The Negroes have offered to help. They've offered their lives."

"If you treat them as equals, Lieutenant, they'll begin to believe it." The colour in Miller's face was rising. "For God's sake! If you let them fight, they'll begin to believe they deserve other liberties. Where would it go from there? Would you have them living here in Sinkler's Ridge? In a house on Main Street?"

Chuckles rippled through the group of townspeople, most of whom had stopped their chatter now to listen in.

Mac once told me integration was the course of the future, the only way.

"You believe peaceful coexistence to be impossible?" I asked, knowing Miller's answer.

"Darn right I do!"

"Joe, calm yourself!" Sally cautioned.

Raines spoke. "Lieutenant, these men, they've never been trained. They'll only get in the way." The objection was a practical one. Raines can always be relied upon for pragmatism. "Besides, at the first shot, they'll run."

"I think you're wrong, Raines," I said plainly.

"*You* are wrong, Lieutenant," Miller argued. "The people of Sinkler's Ridge are of one mind on this issue." He waved a hand to include the observing group of guests.

Heads nodded.

"If you persist in this absurd support of slaves, you'll find that our support will disappear," Miller said stiffly.

Sally turned abruptly and walked from the room. She understood her husband's meaning but obviously did not approve.

"Come, men," I said. Fox and Tweed rose from their chairs. "It seems we've outstayed our welcome."

We left the warm, white house for the cold, black night and walked in silence to the camp.

Spears reported that the pickets had seen nothing but trees in the woods and hills.

I climbed into my narrow makeshift bed and closed my eyes.

All I saw were the colourful foods on the buffet table, the orange fire roaring in the hearth, and Sally's smiling eyes.

And all I heard was music.

JAKE

The more I looked at the makeshift map, the more I realized there weren't going to be any Hork-Bajir left to relocate after the Yeerks came through.

I saw the battle in my mind. I saw the scouts storm the encampment and fire their Dracon beams on everything that moved. I saw the swarm of Taxxons. Hundreds of unstoppable mouths devouring anything with a pulse.

We could slow the Yeerks, inflict sufficient casualties to make the visser in charge look bad. But in the end, defeat was inevitable.

The thought of a total slaughter made me sick.

I had to get away, get another look. Maybe there was something I'd missed.

I morphed peregrine falcon and flew down the valley to the south. The valley was like a wind tunnel. A steady stream of rushing air that kept me aloft almost as well as a thermal.

My raptor eyes caught a flash of movement, something bright and oddly coloured in the forest. I banked and dived, soaring close over the treetops. Through the canopy of leaves and branches, a cluster of tents. Three blue, one green, one yellow, one purple. I banked again and made another pass.

A group of sixteen people. Four adults and a bunch of mostly high-school kids. The campers Tobias had told us about.

I dropped through the trees. I could smell meat cooking, hot dogs I think, and singed marshmallows. I landed and my talons bit firmly into the branch of a fallen tree.

I was less than fifteen metres from the group. I could see everything. Camping equipment scattered everywhere. Metal plates and pans. Boots and wool socks drying on branches. Open rucksacks, spilling their contents of brightly coloured camping gear on to the ground.

Given the amounts of rubbish the campers had strung up in the branches, beyond the reach of bears, they'd been camped for more than three days. Unless these people had portable Kandrona pools in their tiny tents, they weren't Controllers.

I gave in to an irresistible urge to preen and caught the eye of a man in a puffy yellow waistcoat. Watched him magnify and focus a pair of field glasses, then show the kid standing next to him.

I looked directly at them.

We had to get the campers out of there.

I flew up along the edge of the valley and along the crest of the hill north of the colony. Followed the stream that flowed down the valley, through the colony and beyond.

WWHUUMPH!

A small tree toppled. Rustled the under-growth along the stream.

Who would be chopping down trees out here?

I doubled back and landed on the top of a high pine. The small tree had fallen into the water. Not into the rushing stream itself, but into an adjoining pond.

I watched as two small brown heads pushed and tugged on the tree until it moved swiftly through the water towards the edge of the pond. Until it became entangled in a pile of other wood and debris.

One of the animals lumbered up on to the bank. It was a metre long, covered in slick brown fur. A long, flat, paddle-shaped tail dragged along behind it.

Beavers damming the stream.

The wall of wood and undergrowth that held back the pond was leaking. The beavers were working hard to fix it. If the wall broke, all that dammed-up water would rush down the hillside, into the Hork-Bajir colony and on through the valley floor.

It was too good to be true.

A wall of water rushing towards the colony, funnelling towards the attacking Yeerks?

I checked the size of the pond, and the distance the water had to travel to reach the colony and valley floor beyond. . .

No good.

The water in the pond would spread out and diminish by the time it reached the Yeerks. It would spill over the banks of the stream and rage for a while. But where it mattered, it would end up as little more than a puddle.

My brilliant idea began to die. I was about to fly away when the beavers pushed another cluster of tangled branches into position. The wall rose higher. The water level raised ever so slightly.

That's when it hit me.

If two beavers could dam a pond, five beavers could dam a whole lot more.

"We're going to flood them out," I announced. "We're going to wash the Yeerks back down the valley.

"The beavers have already started things for us. We just have to expand their dam to hold back enough water to make a mini tidal wave."

"Nap time!" Marco sang. "I think someone's a *little* overtired."

"I'm fine."

Tobias laughed. <You know, this mission is seriously important. I'm thinking the morph should be a little more, I don't know, glamorous. I mean, going beaver to save an entire colony of aliens is like putting James Bond behind the wheel of a van. With a bumper sticker that says, "World's Greatest Mum". No offence.>

"Very funny. Listen, we've gone mole. We've gone ant. You use what works."

"But will this work?" Rachel asked.

"Got any other ideas?" I answered.

We didn't have to morph to travel to the

beaver dam. It was only about an eight-minute jog up the valley. As we approached the pond. . .

Whack! Whack! Sploosh! Sploosh!

Thundering slaps as loud as firecrackers, and no beavers to be seen. New ripples crossed the pond.

"They must have heard us coming," Cassie said. "Beavers slap their tails on the water if they think they're in danger."

The pond looked promising. It was bigger than it had seemed from the air.

Attached to a lake, it would have made a respectable fishing cove.

In my back garden, it would have made a fantastic swimming-pool.

But I knew we needed more. I just didn't know how much.

<Three to four thousand cubic metres,> Ax said. <I believe that is what it will take to inundate the valley.>

Marco batted his eyelashes. "Ax, you just make me all tingly when you talk all smart-like."

"How much water is that?" I asked.

"We have to make this pool Olympic-sized," Marco answered.

A beaver popped up in the middle of the pond, pushing a branch with his nose. He placed the branch in the dam and dived back underwater.

We waited. And waited.

<Some lungs,> Tobias observed.

"No," Cassie explained, "he's probably in the lodge. See that dome-shaped pile of branches and moss and mud sticking up above water level? There's air in there."

"The lodge?" Marco echoed excitedly. "A roaring fire. Hot chocolate. Britney Spears. Brandy, maybe. The girl, not the drink. These dudes know how to live!"

"The lodge is where they live," Cassie laughed. "Like bears have dens and birds have nests?"

"How do we acquire a beaver while he's inside the lodge?" Rachel said.

Cassie waded into the water. "Well, the entrances are underwater," she said. "Maybe we can catch a beaver on his way out."

She reached the lodge and bent down towards its base. Murky water slapped her chin.

"Found it," she said. "I think. Someone knock lightly on the side of the lodge to scare a beaver out."

"Are you kidding?" Marco said, wading after her into the water. Rachel, Ax and I followed. "Gentle, thoughtful Cassie wants to scare a beaver out of its mind?"

"Shut up and help. I'm not going to hurt him."

Marco tapped the lodge with a fallen branch.

"Got him!" Cassie cried. "Oowwwww! He bit me!"

"Cassie, let go!"

"I'm OK," she said quickly. Then she lifted

the beaver to the surface. His body was still from the acquiring trance, buoyed weight.

Good thing, because this guy had to weigh at least twenty kilos, big and sturdy. The body of an industrious worker. One by one, including Tobias, we reached out to touch the slick, bristly coat.

The beaver splashed away as soon as we had finished.

"You know," Cassie said, forcing a smile, blood dripping from the cut on her hand, "when your mother tells you not to stick your hand in a beaver lodge, you really should listen."

ISAIAH FITZHENRY
December 24, 1864.

Joe Miller's rooster crowed at half past five, leaving no question that it had survived the night despite his predictions of raid and plunder by the Negroes.

While the coffee boiled, I rummaged in my haversack for sugar. I found none, I had to drink my coffee black.

It felt like an ominous omen.

"Don't lag, men. Don't lag!"

Sergeant Spears's husky voice roared through the frigid air. As I made my way across the stream and down the hill, I saw him standing statuesque in the morning fog, having staked out the highest point of the earthworks to supervise Jacob and the other men, who laboured dutifully below.

Spears's rifle was propped against his shoulder. That was as it should have been, for I'd ordered all men to carry arms on every detail.

But from my vantage point, Spears seemed to have his hand rather too close to the trigger.

"They're lazy men, Lieutenant," Spears said, far too loudly, as he saw me approaching. "If our men was out working, we'd have finished by now."

"The problem as I see it, Spears, is that the earth is frozen hard as granite."

"No, sir," Spears said, chuckling, his Scottish accent lengthening his vowels in a most defiant way. "The earth is soft as butter, ain't it, boys? Soft as creamy butter."

Jacob looked up, saw me and dropped his shovel on the ground.

"Lieutenant!" he called, waving an arm and pushing towards me over piles of upturned soil. "I want to speak to you about—"

"You!" Spears bellowed.

Jacob froze.

"Resume your position and your duty!"

Jacob hesitated.

"Lieutenant," he called to me. "It's about the placement of the—"

BAM!

A rifle shot cracked the air.

Jacob hit the ground.

Spears began to chuckle again. He had fired into the sky.

"Spears!" I yelled.

He returned the gun to his shoulder. Jacob staggered to his feet. The eyes of all the black men turned to me.

"Yes, sir?" Spears answered.

"Ride out to scout for the enemy. Take a few men with you."

"Are you relieving me of this detail?"

"I will stand in until your return."

"Very well, sir."

Spears scampered down the earthworks and strode past me in silence. Though he was my subordinate, I couldn't very well question his behaviour in front of the men. I had to back him.

"Back to work, men!" I yelled. "Jacob, approach!" I said sternly and retained a posture of severity until Spears was safely out of earshot.

I sensed the reason Jacob wanted to speak to me. The placement of the entrenchments was all wrong. I'd realized it, too. If we moved them back a hundred yards towards town, we could place them behind the stream, a natural barrier to the Rebs. A God-made moat.

"Jacob," I said gently. "You have an opinion to share?"

He nodded.

"Yes . . . Lieutenant. This ain't the best position. Rebs coming up from down there.

Make 'em come all the way up, close to town. That way, you have more chance to shoot 'em down. Then, when they get to the stream, that slows them down some more."

"I think you're right," I said.

Spears and three privates trampled down the hill on horseback. When they reached the stream, Spears's horse reared up and whinnied loudly.

"Bronco!" Spears cried.

The horse finally plunged into the water, stepping awkwardly over rocks and mud.

Jacob and I exchanged a glance of understanding. The stream was the barrier we needed.

"Start your men digging again," I said. "But this time, according to your plan."

I waited for Jacob to accept the new orders.

"How about rifles?" he said instead, hope flickering in his eyes.

"Why are you so set on fighting? Once you prepare these entrenchments, you can melt back into the hills and be safe. Haven't you heard what these same troopers did at Fort Pillow? Don't you know the name of Nathan Bedford Forrest?"

Jacob's face grew hard and still. He did know the name. But I would drive home the reality.

"Right here in Tennessee, just over those hills a few days, General Forrest's Confederate cavalry captured a Union-held fort on the Mississippi. The Negro soldiers inside surrendered. But

Forrest didn't take them prisoner. He murdered them in cold blood. Jacob, it was a massacre."

"I know, Lieutenant. If they take us, they'll most likely kill us, too."

His calm sent chills down my spine. He knew the truth, yet wanted to fight in spite of it.

"The townspeople won't allow it," I said, changing tack. "Neither will many of my own men. You know Spears. He won't fight beside you."

Jacob looked at me stubbornly.

"You need men," he said, echoing his words from the day before. "Here we are."

I looked angrily at the camp and the town. Didn't Jacob see it was an impossibility? Yes, we were outnumbered. Yes, we needed his men. Yes, it was suicide to turn him down.

"Give us a chance, Lieutenant."

Wagons loaded with household treasures stood outside several houses in town. The white townspeople were loading their possessions and preparing to flee.

I looked at Joe and Sally Miller's house. There was no wagon there.

Clop-clop. Clop-clop. Clop-clop.

The pounding of hooves!

Spears's red and sweating face, flailing coat, and screaming horse reared up before me.

"Lieutenant!" he cried. "They're not a mile from here!"

JAKE

I put Ax in charge of the "dam expansion". He had a clear sense of the mechanics of the whole thing. Said something about how the natural curve of the beaver's dam was actually the most efficient shape to hold back the water.

"Fluid mechanics was one of my specialities as an *aristh*," Ax said.

Marco sighed. "What haven't you done?"

"I have never constructed an organic cellulose hydrological attack assemblage."

"We speak English, dude."

"No, I get it," Rachel said excitedly. "He's never made a dam out of wood, mud and moss."

Cassie was concerned about the beaver family whose compound we were about to take over.

"They're scared. They think we're predators. We need to convince them we're friends."

"What we need to do," Marco said, "is expand this dam and store up a whole lot of water. Fast."

Marco morphed. There was a big splash as he dropped into the water. A resounding crack as he slapped his tail.

<Awesome!> he shouted. <These front teeth are great. Let me at some trees, baby! I'm gonna build me a dam.>

Cassie morphed next. Then Rachel. The beaver was kind of cute, except for the small beady eyes. And the enlarged front incisors, like curving ivory chisels.

I later learned that beaver incisors never stop growing. If the beaver doesn't wear them down with use, they grow right down to the ground.

<There is the beginning of a small canal on the far side of the pond,> Ax said. <It leads to a growth of young trees, some of which have already been cut down. We need that material for the construction. Rachel and Cassie, stay with me. Marco?>

<On my way.>

Tobias and I had other business. I morphed, and together we flew out of range of the construction below. It was a short flight to the campsite. We were careful to land far enough away so that no one would see us demorph and morph in Tobias's case.

Then we walked towards the brightly coloured tents. Thank God we could finally morph some halfway decent clothes, the result of a whole lot of experience. Boys in T-shirts and jeans generally look a lot saner than boys in spandex.

We approached the campsite. A tall kid with glasses spotted us first.

"Hi," he said.

"Hey," I answered.

Then we just stood there.

<Jake? Fearless leader? Do you have a plan,

or are you just going to smile and look stupid in our morphing outfits?> Tobias said privately.

"Just be cool. I'll handle it," I whispered. "I'm Jake," I said to the tall kid.

"Lewis Carpenter. I've had blisters for five days."

"Huh. Bummer."

An adult stuck his head out of a tent. The guy who had sighted me in his binoculars. "What are you two boys doing so far out in the woods?" he asked, stepping outside. "Where's your equipment?"

<Good question, Jake.>

"We're camped on the ridge," I said easily, pointing up the valley wall.

"Right," Tobias added.

More silence and staring. This was getting ridiculous.

"Look," I said. "We came to tell you we all have to get out of here. We just met a ranger and he told us the park is closed. There's a huge storm coming this way. Guy said they're predicting straight-line winds and loads of snow, enough to strand us all. Everyone's got to pack up and get out of the area before sundown."

A girl stood up from the group of kids sitting round the campfire and came closer to us. She was maybe Tom's age.

"It never snows this early in the year."

"Yeah, I know," I said quickly. "That's what's

so dangerous about this storm. No one's prepared. I mean, who's gonna have cold-weather
gear? Right?"

The girl grinned.

"I'll be fine. I hiked Mount McKinley."

"Emily, Lewis?" The adult binocular guy.
"Let me handle this."

<They're not buying it,> Tobias said privately.

"Frostbite is bad news," I said, trying to
sound all serious and worried.

"Look," said binocular guy, "you boys need
to learn a thing or two about hikers' etiquette.
People need to trust one another in the
wilderness. You don't make up stories just to get
someone else's campsite."

The guy held out a tiny portable television
flickering a commercial for a Jeep.

"The local news meteorologist predicts sunny
skies and no wind for the next three days." His
voice bristled with adult annoyance. And with
confidence. "We're staying right where we are."

I could feel my ears getting hot. They turn
red sometimes when I'm embarrassed.

Three more adults, two women and a man,
came from their tents. Asked the kids what was
going on. I started to feel a little ill. Like I was
going to get sent to my room or earn a week's
worth of detention.

"Listen," Tobias said loudly, "you have to
believe us. If you don't get out of this valley

now, something really bad is going to happen. Your lives are in danger."

The campers didn't respond. Emily looked at Lewis, then at the man. A kid near the campfire started to laugh. Pretty soon, all sixteen people in camp were sniggering. Four adults and twelve kids, laughing at the two pathetic losers.

"Get a life," Emily said.

I turned to Tobias. "OK. We're desperate. I don't want to do this, but I don't think we have a choice."

"Are you sure?" Tobias whispered. "What if one of them bolts? Or attacks us? Or runs straight to the local media? If the Yeerks hear that two human boys were morphing. . ."

"I know, Tobias," I snapped. "I know there are consequences."

That was my job. To know the consequences. It was also my job to make the tough decisions. To lead.

I started to morph.

"It's OK," Tobias called. "What you're going to see will shock you, but don't panic. We're only trying to help."

Lewis was the first to react. He clutched at his glasses and stepped back. Groped behind him with his free hand until he bumped into a tree. His mouth hung wide open.

The man dropped his television in the leaves.

His face went white.

One boy by the campfire stumbled to his feet, then took off into the woods.

"Don't be frightened," Tobias repeated.

Morphing is not pretty. It's disturbing and grotesque. Of course the campers were frightened. Anybody would be.

My human body began to twist violently. Big, flesh-tearing teeth sprouted from my gums. Ears migrated to the top of my head. Shoulders hunched, spine expanded, skin toughened. Fur, orange with black stripes, spread across my flesh like liquid spilled out of a jar. Until finally, I fell forward on to the earth. All two hundred kilos of me.

I was a male Siberian tiger standing before a group of whining, whimpering campers, in a place no Siberian tiger should be.

I growled gently. Just enough to let them know the tiger was real.

When Tobias started to demorph, I began to demorph to human.

Emily backed up, tripped, fell to the forest floor. Tears streaked her face.

The red-tailed hawk shrieked once, then morphed to human.

"Who . . . what are you?" the man cried.

"Its a long story," I said, fully human again. "I can't explain it all now, but you've got to believe we're not here to hurt you."

The campers were silent. At least no one else ran.

"Sometime before tomorrow noon," I said solemnly, "an army of aliens is going to march up this valley. If you're still here, they'll kill every single one of you."